Mixter-Maxter

Fireside tales from Orkney

Mixter-Maxter first published in 2006
by Margaret Stevenson Headley
Stymilders
Stenness
Orkney KW17 2JY

Many of the stories in this volume previously
appeared in *The Orcadian* or *The Orkney View*.
A previous volume, *The Voldro's Nest*, was
published by The Orkney Press in 1986.

Printed by The Orcadian Ltd
Hell's Half Acre
Hatston
Kirkwall
Orkney KW15 1DW

ISBN 0-9552705-0-2

Mixter-Maxter

Fireside tales from Orkney

written and illustrated by
Margaret Stevenson Headley

Dedication

For my children
Kate, Nina, Bob, Ruth, Karen and Tony

My grandchildren
Carol, Iain, Michael, Donald, Rachel, Craig,
Leigh, Paul and Ross

My great grandchildren
Rhiannon, Dylan, Ruby, Robert and Jack

Acknowledgements

My thanks to Marion Hamilton who started the ball rolling,
to my daughter Karen who typed the script
and to Pam Beasant and Iain Ashman who pulled it all together.

I am also grateful to the Orkney Islands Council, for financial
assistance towards the production of this book.

"Come," called the teller of tales.
"Come my children, come sit by me in the ingle and I
will tell you tales of the wild wind, cold from the
ice caves of the North, warm from the
buttercup meadows and the island shores.
Come listen. Sit by me."

Contents

Foreword

Yin Ting Pookiness 1

A New Home for Vernon Vole 3

A Goat in the Garden 7

The Muckle Spider 10

Eggstraspecial 12

Buried Treasure 14

A Likely Story 17

A Hunting We Will Go 20

The Stolen Baby 23

The Spangled Starlings 26

Dandelions 28

The Feather Pillow 30

A Dog's Life 33

The Green Gnome 37

Of Mice and Many 40

One Good Turn 47

Calamity 49

The Fire Dragon 51

All for One 53

Hare-on-the-Hill 55

The Treasure Box 57

The Bouncing Ball 60

An Odd Fellow 63

The Eel Well 66

The Silver Bridle 69

None for the Pot 72

Coral Creechurs 74

The Large Brown Mouse 76

The Keelieworm 79

The Sly Goose 83

The Silver Fishes 85

Transportation 87

The Lickull Piggie 91

Day Trip 105

The Peedie Herdie Boy 109

The Great North Wind 112

The March of the Snowmen 115

Winter 118

To Celebrate the Birthday 121

The Shepherd Boy's Flute 125

Glossary 129

Foreword

If you are about to read this book you are in for a treat. It's a little gem and the writing of Margaret Stevenson Headley is one of Orkney's hidden treasures. We have had glimpses of her work in *The Orcadian* and *The Orkney View*; this is a collection of stories gathered from both publications along with some recent work.

Margaret spent her childhood on the island of Stronsay where much of her free time was spent roaming among the hills and heather. Her aptitude for storytelling reflects her love of nature and her empathy with all that is around her. Her ability to imagine the thoughts and fears of a field mouse or the bargaining powers of a sandlo endear her as a fine storyteller.

Her style is a beautiful marriage of dialect, folklore and imagination.

I have always loved stories. Listening to them, reading them or telling them to children. I love these stories, and so have the children I have read them to.

Whether it be a peedie Sandlo, a Groolie Belkie or a vole, these encounters happened a long time ago, or maybe it was only yesterday. Their essence captures the fields and shores, streams and ditches of the Orkney Islands. Listen to what you hear. Look at what you see. Realise that the characters from these tales are all around you with more stories to tell.

Marion Hamilton

Yin Ting Pookiness

Yin Ting Pookiness had been shut outside again. He
climbed up onto the windowsill and peered into the sitting
room but no one was about. The fire was switched off
and the morning coffee mugs stood emptily around. Just
because there had been a brief blink of sunshine, they had
all gone off to work and left him outside. To get the good
of the sun, they said, but he much preferred to be indoors,
sleeping on his blanket in the bottom oven of the stove.

Presently, the milkman came up the road in his
yellow van, with the milk bottles a-clatter in their crates,
and when he got down to leave the day's milk in the back
porch, Yin Ting Pookiness sneaked stealthily by him, and
contrived to get shut in.

Not that it was as cosy as the kitchen, but there was
a warm patch of sunlight falling through the window, and
he basked in that till late morning, washing his brown ears
and polishing his long thin tail till it shone like a liquorice
stick.

A fat bluebottle came buzzing up against the
window. Yin Ting Pookiness leapt about trying to catch
him, making some nasty rents in the window curtains
and on the sleeve of a yellow oilskin jacket hanging on the
back of the door. Pretty soon he captured the bluebottle,
peeled off his wings and scrunched him up delicately, then
looked around for some other diversion.

A box of seedlings stood in the corner waiting to be
planted out, so he dug around in that for a time, carefully
scooping all the damp earth out of the box and spreading

1

it over the floor. The nemesias and pansies he tossed back into the empty box where they wilted and died.

After a time, he heard the postman come whistling up the path, and two or three letters dropped through the letterbox.

Yin Ting Pookiness bounded across and quickly sorted through the envelopes, choosing a long blue one from the bank, which he shredded up meticulously, leaving only the stamp intact. He flew about among the paper bits, scattering them like confetti all over the floor, and then he climbed up to the narrow window ledge and looked out on to the road where the common hayshed cat was lounging in the sun with her kittens. He tapped on the glass till the kittens came to see, and then glared so ferociously at them with his crossed blue eyes that they ran away in a fright and hid among the long grass.

At last, he heard the voices of the children coming up the road from school, and Dad's car trundling into the garage. The kitchen door was unlocked, a generous portion of fish was ladled into the blue dish by the sink, and the fire switched on in the sitting room.

Yin Ting Pookiness ate his fish and had a long drink of water from the wash basin in the bathroom, then he strolled through to the sitting room and sharpened his claws on the back of the big chair by the fire.

He stretched himself on the rug. Fresh air and the great outdoors were all very well, but give him the fireside every time.

A New Home for Vernon Vole

Vernon Vole had been asleep for only an hour or so when disaster befell him. His first thought, when he heard the heavy footsteps overhead, was that Nimrod, the Great White Cat, had at last discovered where he had built his snug abode, but when a succession of loud thumps reverberated through his little house, and the walls actually began to bulge and heave, he realised that this was not Nimrod's style at all, since that animal was inclined to sneak up with extreme stealth, before pouncing on innocent voles. Perhaps his home had been struck by lightning? Only last week his grandmother's postillion had been thus afflicted, but since no trace of the unfortunate creature had ever been found, other than a very bent post horn, Vernon was not at all certain of the symptoms of the occurrence.

He soon dismissed both these eventualities, when, to his horror, the entire ceiling disappeared, and he was left exposed in his little grassy bed, clutching himself in fright as the harsh daylight flooded into his room. For a dreadful moment he was transfixed, gazing upwards to where he could see a monstrous giant peering down at him. The giant was wearing green trousers, a purple hat and heavy boots, and in his hand he held a large spade.

"Oh dear," said the giant, in a very apologetic tone. "I am so dreadfully sorry to have disturbed you. I was about to plant this tree." He indicated a rather withered sycamore, which lay on the grass beside him.

"Plant a tree!" Vernon was beginning to recover from his fright and discover that he was really quite angry. He had gone to such pains to select a really private spot for his house, away out in the middle of the buttercup meadow, and here was this giant, blundering about planting trees in the very same spot. Really, it was too bad.

"Plant a tree!" he repeated, his voice quite squeaky with alarm. He clasped his hands together so that the giant would not notice that they were trembling, and took a deep breath. "I have no wish to have a tree planted anywhere *near* my house. The roots would be a positive nuisance, getting into everything, and no doubt it would introduce all sorts of undesirable characters to the neighbourhood. *Owls* even!" Here Vernon Vole became so agitated that he felt quite faint and had to close his eyes for a spell. While he was recovering the giant shuffled around uncomfortably, taking his cap off and putting it on again several times, before he finally spoke.

"Is there anything I can do to repair the damage?" He picked up a large piece of turf and passed it aimlessly from hand to hand as he considered how best it might be returned to its original position. "Perhaps this could be utilized?"

Vernon raised his eyes heavenwards. "Don't be ridiculous. This establishment was the work of months. You can't just tear it to bits and then expect to effect a repair with any old lump of earth. It will take the rest of the summer to put everything in order again." His contemplation of the task suddenly overwhelmed Vernon, and he leaned his head in his hands.

The giant was mortified. His quiet morning's gardening had turned out to be quite disastrous, and now here was this poor vole, a harmless enough fellow, faced with the stupendous task of having to rebuild his entire home. No wonder he was upset.

"Now I come to think of it," the giant began hesitantly. "Whilst I was digging farther down the field I chanced upon rather a fine piece of drainpipe. With the minimum of trouble I suspect it could be converted into a very substantial residence. Wait here and I'll go and fetch it."

He hastily threw down his spade and set off at a smart pace towards the lower end of the buttercup meadow, returning a few minutes later bearing a length of grey piping.

Vernon regarded the pipe with grudging approval. "I don't think I care much for the colour," he said at last, feeling obliged not to appear too eager, but secretly he was thinking to himself that it would make a much better house than his original residence. It would be completely wind and waterproof and, more importantly, impervious to attacks from marauding creatures such as Nimrod, the Great White Cat, or even the Owls.

With the giant's assistance, the piece of pipe was positioned at a slight slope on a bed of pebbles, so that any water that might seep in would drain quickly away, and by the time Vernon had collected his supply of warm bedding from the wreck of his old home, the new dwelling was complete.

Later that evening, after the giant had departed to plant his tree farther afield, Vernon sat basking in the slanting rays of the setting sun, where they fell warm across his new doorstep. Taken all round, it had been an adventurous day. All had been for the best, like many another thing.

A Goat in the Garden

Once upon a time, on a brave May morning, the Muckle Grullyan roused himself from his bed and looked out at the day.

It was a splendid morning to be sure. The sun was up and the wind was down, the larks were in the high clouds shouting their heads off. In the daisy-white meadows the new lambs galloped like crazy. The hens were singing at their morning's egg-laying. In short, it was a morning to be up and doing, and what the Muckle Grullyan needed to be doing, amongst other things, was his garden.

There it lay in the sun, choked with weeds, littered with empty bottles and tins which had overflowed from the rubbish bins, bristling with pots of tar, bits of frayed rope, old iron and coils of rusty wire. It was anything but a garden. Something would have to be done at once, before it got completely out of hand, so as soon as he had eaten his breakfast, the Muckle Grullyan went into his shed to look out his spade and fork, and the trowel with the bent handle. Then he began to dig, stopping every so often to think about this and that, planning a bit of crazy paving here and there, and maybe a rose by the wall, and marigolds of course. They would grow if nothing else would.

So the day went by; and when evening came the Muckle Grullyan found that he had really made very little progress. There was more to this gardening than met the eye. What he needed was a little help, but that wasn't so easily come by, and if he did get help he might even have to pay for it, and that hardly bore thinking about.

Presently he had a splendid notion. He'd get a goat to eat all the long grass and stuff in the middle of the garden, while he laid out a nice border all round, and in that way he'd have a smooth green lawn kept constantly trimmed, while all he would need to do would be to look after the border all round the edges, which surely wouldn't amount to much more than a bit of gentle weeding and snipping off a withered bloom here and there.

Accordingly, at first light next morning, he was off to get himself a goat, from the Nokh who lived over the Great Heathery Hill, and who kept a large flock of the hairy creatures.

After a deal of trouble they finally captured the skinniest one of the whole flock, but the Muckle Grullyan thought that this might be all to the good, as the animal looked ravenous and would be sure to eat all the more.

As soon as they got home, the goat was tethered firmly in the middle of the garden by a stout rope, where it immediately began tearing up huge mouthfuls of greenery and gobbling them down almost as quickly as a combine harvester. All very pleasant, thought the Muckle Grullyan to himself, as he pottered among his plants in the border, and watched the goat cleaning up the wilderness in the middle.

In no time at all the garden began to look quite neat, with the flowers blooming handsomely along the edges, and a few shrubs spreading green by the wall.

The goat by this time was beginning to get a bit low on grass, but that was just his hard luck, as the Muckle Grullyan remarked laughingly to him. If the worst came to the worst, he might toss him a cabbage leaf or two to keep him going, but there was no hurry on that. So thought the Muckle Grullyan as he laid by his gardening tools for the day.

He felt quite differently next morning however, when he discovered the goat had finished off all the grass and had gone right on eating, first his tether and then on to the flower beds, which he had stripped clean down to the roots. He was just getting yokit into the clothes lines, complete with pegs and thermal underwear, when the Muckle Grullyan appeared on the scene in a very nasty frame of mind indeed.

Which only goes to show that, although it may be a bit more bother, perhaps it is better to do your own turn in the long run.

The Muckle Spider

Once upon a time there was a muckle great spider. High in the corner of the neep shed, just above the great door, he had spun for himself a fine web, which swung and glistered in the sunlight that slanted in through the high door.

Each day he added a new strand, till the shining net stretched enticingly for nearly a yard on every side, and each day he retired to the darkest corner, keeping a firm hold on the last silken thread so that if some gauzy insect became entangled in the web, he'd feel the shaking, and then he'd hurry down through the gossamer threads to see what he had caught. If it was a big matlo and too much to eat all at once he'd wrap it in silk threads and carry it up to his larder to keep for a rainy day, but if it was a peedie mudgie or the like he'd gobble it up in a trice.

So the days passed well enough, but the muckle great spider was not really happy because he had no one to talk to, and not one friend in the whole wide world. The white doves, flying in and out through the open door to their nests up in the aisons had no time to stop and speak, always they were busy with their own affairs and could not be bothered with the muckle great spider. The peedie grey mice, collecting hay seeds from the floor, squeaked and squabbled among themselves but never spared a glance for the lonely spider. He even tried to make friends with the farmer's wife when she came in for a neep for dinner, lowering himself down on a gossamer strand and bumping hopefully against her cheek, but she only screamed in fright and beat at him with her basket. Sadly he resigned himself to his lonely life, high up in the dark corner.

One day a shiny red tractor roared up to the shed with a load of neeps, and after much to-ing and fro-ing it empied the heap into a corner of the shed and roared off once more about its business.

After the noise had died away and the doves settled back on to their nests, the muckle great spider became aware of a tiny peedie voice calling and crying for help. The muckle great spider peered about this way and that, but his eyesight was not all that good, so he lowered himself carefully down on a silken thread till he came near to the pile of neeps, and there he spied a poor black gablo pinned by the leg under a large neep.

The muckle great spider thought and thought of ways and means to free the poor old black gablo. He spun out yards of filmy cobweb, around and about the neep, and from here to there across and along till after much tugging and pulling on this thread and that, he finally succeeded in raising the neep just a fraction, but enough to let the old black gablo free himself. Then was the gablo no' delighted! He galloped about flexing his legs to make sure no permanent injury had been done, and then they sat in the sun on a big stone, chatting of this and that, and the muckle great spider thought to himself how pleasant it was to have someone to talk to, even although it was only an old black gablo.

Eggstraspecial

Once upon a time there was a bowl of brown eggs standing on a shelf in the pantry, and after a time they began to wonder what was to become of them.

"I shall be an omelette," boasted the largest egg, "simply smothered in bits of bacon, and tomato, and mushrooms, all brown and golden and delicious." He was extremely self-important, and had arranged himself on the very top of the bowl.

"I should like to be baked in a cake," declared another egg. "What?" cried the largest egg, "and become mixed up with all those common currants? I shouldn't fancy that." "I should like to be poached," cried a little egg from the bottom of the bowl. "Huh!" scoffed the largest egg, "I knew you'd get yourself into hot water some day." "I'd prefer to be lightly boiled and eaten with toasty fingers of bread," said a big fat egg. "You could do worse," agreed the largest egg.

"We'd much rather be meringues," twittered two silly little eggs on the rim of the bowl. "And waste two perfectly good yolks?" remarked the largest egg bitterly. "That is just so typical of you extravagant pair. Think what you could do with two lovely yellow yolks: pop them in a salad dressing or fish cakes, or soup, even." "Soup?" cried all the eggs in a chorus, "we never ever heard of egg soup." "Well you have now," pointed out the largest egg in a grand manner. "In fact, I shouldn't be at all surprised if that's how you ended up. In egg soup!" And he began to laugh in a very vulgar manner.

12

"You are deliberately upsetting us," said one of the eggs bravely. "No good ever comes of teasing, you'll see."

Just then the fat cook came busily into the pantry. "Take me!" cried all the eggs in a chorus, and the largest egg stretched himself up to his full height to be noticed first, but he stretched up too far and over he toppled down on to the shelf with a sickening crunch, and his insides ran away over the edge and dripped heavily on to the floor.

"Tsk! Tsk!" complained the cook, as she swept him up and threw him into the waste bin. "Now I shall be short of an egg, but never mind," she went on as she gathered the rest of them into her apron, "eleven eggs will do just as well as twelve to set under my broody hen."

And so they did.

When all the eggs had hatched out, the baby chickens were left to run free in the green meadow. "How pleasant," said the two smallest chicks. Much nicer than being a meringue," and they chased a cloud of little black flies through the tall grass.

Buried Treasure

The Muckle Grullyan was digging laboriously in his potato patch. It seemed to be harder than ever this year, and he leaned more and more heavily on the spade each time he came to the end of the row.

The ducks came flapping round his feet, gobbling the long pink worms as if they were spaghetti. "What a pity ducks cannot dig," thought the Muckle Grullyan. A pig, now, would be most useful for digging out the more deep rooted weeds like the dochans, and that troublesome thistle with the roots that went down as far as the Great Barrier Reef. Likely it would take a deal of time and patience to teach a pig to dig in neat, straight rows, anyway. It could not be done in less than a month, or even longer, and the potato patch needed to be dug right now.

The Muckle Grullyan sighed heavily and bent once more to the spade. All at once his eye was caught by a bright gleam in the earth. Could it possibly be a gold coin? He'd heard of such a thing. A casket full of gold coins dug up thousands of years after being hidden in the soil. He threw aside his spade and began to sift through the damp earth. There it was again! Was it a coin? Alas, it was only part of a milk bottle top, and he threw it away in disgust, picking up his spade once more.

Then he had an idea! If it became known that there was a hidden hoard of gold in his potato patch it was very likely that every person within miles would be round hot foot with a spade to dig. He must give them a message.

As luck would have it, the Nokh from over the Great Heathery Hill was passing at that very moment, and the Muckle Grullyan suddenly uttered a loud cry and pretended to pick up a coin from the half-dug earth. Actually it was a half crown that he had had in his pocket for some time, hoping to pass it off as a ten-penny piece when a suitable opportunity arose.

The Nokh was properly impressed and swallowed the tale of hidden treasure with alacrity. He dashed off home for a spade, spreading the glad tidings as he went, and in less than no time a crowd descended upon the Muckle Grullyan's potato patch, with forks and spades and rakes and hoes, and began digging like maniacs.

The Muckle Grullyan was careful to drop a coin from time to time, just to whet their appetites, so to speak, and since it was only half a dozen old halfpennies he wasn't really wasting anything, and, as the crowd said between bursts of digging, where one coin was, there were sure to be others.

"I say," said the Nokh after a time. "What happens when we do find the treasure? I hope we won't be expected to share it!" "Share it?" cried the Muckle Grullyan, laughing lightly. "Don't be ridiculous! Finders keepers, that's the rule here."

Suddenly a great shout went up from a crowd of peedie buckies who were digging like crazy among the roots of an old bhour tree by the wall. "We've found the treasure! We've found the treasure!" And before the astonished, not to say chagrined, gaze of the Muckle

Grullyan, they dragged out a tin box, oozing gold coins from a rusty hole in the side.

"How could such a thing be possible," wailed the Muckle Grullyan, as he watched the peedie buckies gleefully making off with their prize over the rim of the hill.

He went over to dig hopefully once more under the old tree, but there was nothing there. He lifted his spade onto his shoulder and trudged back to the potato patch. Time was getting on.

A Likely Story

Once upon a time there was a family of spiders. There was Father Spider, Mamma Spider, five baby spiders, Granny Spider, Aunt Esmeralda Spider, Uncle Septimus Spider and Fred the cabin boy, and they all lived together in the top of a very tall house.

In fact it was so very near the top that it was actually the rafters, and although it was quite warm, because of course heat always rises, it was a teeny bit inconvenient in some ways. Like, for instance, Mamma Spider might be speeding through from the kitchen with the tea tray piled high with honey buns and flies' legs when down she would fall between two rafters and only some very smart web work would save her from rather a sticky end.

Luckily she had once been a trapeze artiste so she was not so inconvenienced as someone else might have been, but after a time she began to suffer quite badly on account of her nerves and Aunt Esmeralda took over some of the cooking.

This would have been an admirable solution to the food problem but for the fact that Aunt Esmeralda had become quite faddy about her meals and had embarked on a vegetarian diet, and all that healthy food lark. Carrot juice and charcoal biscuits for breakfast. You know the sort of thing. So her cooking was not all that eagerly sought after. Granny Spider used to help out, but she was getting past it, poor old soul, and you never knew what she'd put in the pot by mistake. Somebody's socks disappeared rather mysteriously and the bits in the soup could have been tomato, as she said, but whoever saw blue tomatoes?

Cleaning also presented quite a problem, for no matter how carefully they swept and dusted some bits of refuse were almost bound to escape and plunge down into the flat beneath, and this led to somewhat strained relations with the occupants of that particular quarter, who happened to be a colonel and his wife, and you know what the army is like as regards filth. Everything in their place was whitewashed, including the coal, and the colonel was constantly upstairs, beating on the door of the spiders' apartment, bellowing about infamous behaviour, horse whipping, courts martial and other evils. The final blow fell, as you might say, when young Fred the cabin boy upset the bowl of piranha fish. Luckily they dropped into the colonel's bath where they were speedily captured, not however, before they had devoured the loofah and two tablets of carbolic soap. All in all, it was becoming apparent that a proper floor would have to be installed with the utmost speed.

The spiders, of course, were in their usual impecunious state, and after a deal of deliberation it was decided to have a quick whip round among the neighbours, and the entire family set out with a hand cart to see what they could collect in the way of flooring. As might have been expected, they drew a complete blank, and they sat around despondently on the front steps for another think.

Uncle Septimus, who had been gazing up into the branches of a nearby oak tree suddenly smote his forehead and sprang to his feet. He had been taking Karate lessons all winter and here was a golden opportunity to show off his prowess. He advanced upon the king of the forest, and, with a few well-aimed blows, the tree was felled and he began cutting it into neat sections which the spiders quickly ferried upstairs and arranged in neat rows along the rafters. Spiders of course are almost as notorious as ants regarding hard work, so that the floor was laid almost as soon as the tree was cut down.

Granny produced some fine spun rugs which she'd laid by just in case, and with those spread around, the top flat took on quite a sumptuous air. With the laying of the floor, the colonel automatically acquired a new roof, and he became almost jovial, actually sending up a spare bucket of whitewash to freshen the walls as well. Which only goes to show that necessity is indeed the mother of invention.

A Hunting We Will Go

Chiko and Yin Ting Pookiness were waiting by the
blue dish for their breakfast. They were not really very
hungry and when the Mistress spooned out the meat
they only nibbled delicately at the edges and hardly ate
a thing. "Spoilt cats," said the Mistress. "You should
be out hunting instead of having all these delicacies
placed in front of you," and she hurried off to do her
housework.

Chiko and Yin Ting Pookiness washed their faces
and polished their long brown tails, and then
decided all of a sudden to see the world, and perhaps
find a mouse to eat. Out into the bright morning they

sallied, through the wire fence and down into the high
grasses of the long meadow.

It was cool and dark among the grass, with the
wind rustling the tall stems, and they crept slowly along,
their blazing blue eyes looking this way and that, and

their brown ears twitching to catch the sound of a voldro or the twitter of a bird in the thicket; but not a whisper did they hear. They climbed a wall by the way, and Chiko pounced upon a big black slug sitting on a leaf in the shade, but got nothing for his pains save a covering of sticky slime on his paws, and a horrid taste in his mouth.

A brown rat shambled out of a deep crack in the wall, and Chiko and Yin Ting Pookiness lay as still as death, watching and waiting while the old brown rat nibbled an ear of corn, and looked about him with evil red eyes. Yin Ting Pookiness arranged his long brown legs ready to spring, and then, with the merest twitch of his tail, he pounced upon the old brown beast, sinking his sharp teeth into the rat's neck. But the rat was not to be so easily caught, and he bit Yin Ting Pookiness cruelly, right on the tip of his ear, so that he let him go at once, shaking his head to ease the pain, and the brown rat scampered swiftly back into the cleft in the wall.

The two cats sat down in the shelter of a gorse bush and had a think, and Chiko washed his paws, and cleaned his brown face. The day was getting late and still they had not caught a morsel to eat. Perhaps there might be a rabbit asleep among the grassy tussocks below the brae, so they set off once more through the slanting shadows, and down into the valley, but the rabbits were away and gone, and only a swift hare crossed their path, running like the wind into the great wide yonder.

Chiko and Yin Ting Pookiness climbed slowly homeward. A butterfly hovered overhead and Chiko sprang hopefully to catch him, but only a sprinkling of silvery dust from the gauzy wings caught on the kitten's whiskers, and made him sneeze.

The two cats squeezed carefully under the wire fence and padded softly in through the open door of the kitchen. The blue dish stood waiting, full to the brim, and they ate every scrap. Then they washed their faces and ears and polished their long brown tails until they shone. They stretched and yawned and curled themselves tightly together in a furry ball, with their long brown legs folded round each other's necks, and they went to sleep.

The Stolen Baby

Once upon a time, far away over the moss, and close by the Great Heathery Hill, there was a peedie cottage. It had a turf roof with a window that looked right up into the sky. Here lived a man and his wife.

Their dearest wish was for a baby of their own, and after many years their wish came true, and a baby girl was born to them. She was the loveliest baby you had ever seen, with the bluest eyes and the curliest hair. Her mother and father loved her, and could not bear to be parted from her even for a day, so they took her with them everywhere they went, even when they went to work in the fields. The mother would wrap her in a warm blanket and put her in her basket in the shade of the prickly thorn bush, and there she'd lie all day till the sun set and it was time to go home.

One day, when the sun was high, the mother looked to where her baby's basket lay under the thorn bush. She thought she saw a shadow move beneath the bush, so she laid down her hoe and went to see if her baby was still asleep. As she drew near the basket she noticed that the blanket had been moved, and when she peeped beneath it she saw that her baby was no longer there. In her place was an ugly shrivelled infant, its face all twisted with crying.

The poor mother was heartbroken, for she knew at once that a wicked Hilly Trow had stolen her baby and left this ugly infant in its place. She hunted among the bushes and rocks, but not a sign of her lovely baby could she find, and soon it began to get dark, so she picked up the basket with the ugly screaming infant inside, and went sadly home.

All night long she wondered how she could find her baby, till at last, when the sky began to grow light, she decided to go and see the Old Wise Wife and ask her what she should do. As soon as she had fed the ugly screaming infant she set off over the stony brae.

Soon she came to the dark house where the Old Wise Wife lived, and knocked on the door. The old woman was not very pleased to see a visitor so early in the morning, but when the poor mother explained what had happened she listened very carefully and sat thinking for a long time. She knew that the Hilly Trow would not give up such a lovely baby without a great deal of trouble.

At last she remembered that the Hilly Trow loved to eat the fat blaeberries that grew on the Great Heathery Hill; but he was too lazy to look for them himself, for they were hard to find. If the mother could gather enough to please him, perhaps he would exchange them for her golden-haired baby. So she set off at once over the stony brae till she came to the Great Heathery Hill. All day she hunted for the fat blaeberries among the heather, till at last she had enough.

Next morning, as soon as it was daylight, she picked up the basket with the ugly screaming infant inside, and carrying the bag of blaeberries, she set off to find the Hilly Trow. Many a weary mile she trudged, looking hopefully this way and that for the dark cave where the Hilly Trow lived.

She came upon a clump of white heather with its

24

pale leaves shining, so she picked a sprig and laid it among the berries. At last, when she was feeling so tired that she had almost given up, she came to the bleak stony hill, and there was the Hilly Trow's cave.

As she came nearer, she could see the wicked Hilly Trow sitting in the entrance, and he glared at her through his long rough hair. She laid the basket with the ugly infant in it at his feet, and showed him the bag of fat blaeberries. He knew at once why she had come, and looked greedily at the juicy berries, then he disappeared into the darkness of the cave. In a short time he came back carrying her sleeping baby, and placed it safe and sound in her arms once more.

She wrapped it closely in its own warm blanket and started for home, back down the stony brae, and the wicked Hilly Trow troubled them no more.

The Spangled Starlings

Once upon a time, high in the aisons of the big garage, two bold spangled starlings built a fine nest of dry grasses and wisps of wool and hair.

Here the mother starling laid four blue-green eggs and for many days the parent birds shared the task of keeping the eggs warm till at last, one fine morning, the first fledgling broke through the slender shell. Soon the four baby birds had hatched out and the two spotted starlings were kept busy all the long day carrying grubs and insects to feed their clamouring babies.

At last, when they were nearly three weeks old the mother starling decided it was time for the four young ones to leave the high nest and learn to fly and hunt for food for themselves, so the baby birds made their first venture into the air, blundering clumsily from one ledge to another, until they could fly for quite a long distance in the shelter of the big garage.

One of the baby birds, which was larger and more adventurous than the others, flew boldly outside the wide door and perched unsteadily on a rusty iron rail. For a time he swung happily in the warm sun, but as he prepared to launch himself once more into the little breeze that blew along the wall, a dreadful thing happened. He dropped heavily into a large tin of thick oil waste. His fuzzy baby feathers quickly soaked up the thick oil and the more he struggled the farther he sank into the black mess. He had just given himself up for lost when by some lucky chance a peedie girl came by and spied the baby bird almost drowned in the thick oil. She lifted him up and wrapped him in a large green leaf and carried him indoors to her mother where he was washed gently in warm soapy water. At first he struggled bravely, splashing the new yellow wallpaper with oily water, but soon he lay quite still, the grey shutters closed down over his bright eyes, while the green soapy liquid was rubbed carefully into his feathers and the black oil was washed off and rinsed away.

The draggled bundle of feathers was dried gently in a soft cloth and he was placed outside on the lid of the water tank to dry in the sun.

At first, he clung tightly to the tin lid with his eyes closed, but soon his feathers began to dry out and he gave a little chirp and hopped a short distance along the lid. Then, with another chirp he shook out his peedie wings and flew across the lawn into the high garden wall where he perched carefully among the grey stones.

His cries were soon heard by the two parent birds and they swooped round him, carrying grubs and insects, and in a little while the baby bird followed them safely back across the garden to join the rest of the hungry brood in the aisons of the big garage.

Dandelions

Once upon a time there was an old stone quarry with a great grinding machine alongside, where the stones were crushed and broken into tiny pieces for mending the roads and such like. The steep sides of the quarry were covered in dust and grime and oily puddles streamed across the bottom among the piles of stone and rubble.

After many years, the old stone quarry fell into disuse and a great silence hung over its stone walls. Only the wind and rain blew chill in this bleak and desolate place.

Then one day a fluff of dandelion seed came drifting and gliding in on the wind and was swirled into a dusty cranny where it lay all through the long winter. When spring came, and the sun shone down into the old stone quarry, the dandelion seed began to send out tiny little roots into the warm dust around it, and then it unfolded a single frail leaf and looked out at the world. A sad and dreary world to be sure, with not a green leaf except its own, nor even a bird to sing in the silence. Only grey walls stretching into the sky, with the scattered rocks drowning in the black puddles at their feet.

All through the spring and summer the dandelion grew and flourished, spreading its green leaves on the warm earth, and hoisting its golden crown on a long thick stem. And all through the spring and summer it watched and waited in vain for someone to share its lonely life, but never a one came to the old stone quarry, except for a fat striped bee, bumbling by in the summer dusk, laden with nectar for the hive. He stopped to rest on the yellow dandelion, but only for a little while, before the dark night came down; and when he had gone, the dandelion felt lonelier than ever, though he stood bravely, strong and tall.

Summer turned to autumn, and the dandelion's golden crown grew silvery white, and drooped over the tall stem, till the cold winter came with icy winds and blew the feathery seeds in scattered drifts over the grey rubble. The poor dandelion folded his shrivelled leaves in the bitter wind and went to sleep.

As it will, spring came round once more, and once more the dandelion sent out new roots into the warm earth, and once more it unfolded a green leaf and looked around. There, on every side, the green leaves of a hundred tiny dandelions were spread in the cool shadows, clinging in the dusty crannies, and leaning amongst the pebbles.

As the days went by and the sun shone warmly into the old stone quarry, the dandelions grew and flourished, hoisting their golden crowns till they spread in a yellow pool over the rubble, like a light in the dark.

The Feather Pillow

Once upon a time, far and away across the Great North Sea, there lived a Peedie Sandlo, and all day long and all day long he spundered here and there among the rocks, looking for tit-bits among the chingle and the ware.

One day as he searched among the buckies and the stones, he came upon the Great Groolie Belkie sitting by the side of a deep pool. He was leaning his head on his hand and gazing sorrowfully into the green water.

"Ho there, Groolie Belkie," cried the Peedie Sandlo, "is there anything wrong?"

The Groolie Belkie heaved a great sigh and said sadly: "Yes, indeed. I feel so tired, but try as I will, I just cannot get any sleep. All night long I toss and turn, but never a wink of sleep do I get."

The Peedie Sandlo was very sorry to hear this, and suggested that the Great Groolie Belkie should try a hot drink with a sprinkling of nutmeg before bedtime, or perhaps a brisk walk, or even counting sheep, but the Great Groolie Belkie had tried them all to no avail.

At last the Peedie Sandlo decided that they should go and visit the Old Wise Wife who lived far and away across the Great Heathery Hill, so they both set off to ask her advice.

Soon they reached her lonely cottage and they waited patiently until she had collected her thoughts. It would not be easy to find a cure, she said, and the best one she could think of was to make a pillow and fill it with feathers and down. But it must be very special feathers, because they must be collected from Mother Carey's Chickens, and as everyone knows, Mother Carey's Chickens fly forever away and away out across the Great North Sea, only resting at night, and sleeping afloat on the wide dark water. Nevertheless, the Great Groolie Belkie felt sure they could find them, and such kind gentle birds would be certain to give them a wisp of feathers and down.

That very night, just as the darkness began to fall, they set off, launching the Great Groolie Belkie's wicker boat onto the dark ocean. The Peedie Sandlo stood high in the sharp end, holding aloft a flickering lantern, while the Great Groolie Belkie rowed mightily on the oars.

Far and away they sailed, following the silvery moon trail out onto the Great North Sea, and far and away they sailed all through the night, until at last, just as the pale pearly light of morning began to creep into the sky, they came upon a flotilla of Mother Carey's Chickens swinging at anchor on the surface of the sea, and just waking up to begin the new day.

They listened carefully to the Great Groolie Belkie's sad story and soon collected enough feathers and down to fill a large pillow, and the Great Groolie Belkie and the Peedie Sandlo turned once more towards home.

Tired and weary, they reached the shore and set to work at once to make a pillow, stitching and sewing till at last it was finished, and the Great Groolie Belkie placed it carefully in his bed and lay down.

No sooner had his head touched the pillow than he fell fast asleep, and he slept and he slept and he slept.

And the Peedie Sandlo wandered away slowly back home, climbing over the rocks and ware and looking for titbits among the chingle.

A Dog's Life

Cassie Putt was walking along the top of the stone wall that ran around the farmyard. His black velvet feet made not a sound as he came towards the gate where Muffin's kennel stood. The kennel was red and above the door was a sign that said "MUFFIN: MERCILESS DOG". Cassie Putt stopped and peered down at the sign, and as he did so a small pebble dislodged itself from the wall and fell noisily to the ground. Instantly a small bundle of hair erupted from the door of the kennel, snapping and snarling and leaping about in all directions at once as far as its chain would allow, pausing at last to ascertain that no one was there. There it stood still, feet planted firmly on the ground and glared ferociously around, breathing heavily.

Cassie Putt sat quite still, high up on the wall, until Muffin finally spotted him. "Was that you," snapped Muffin, "heaving stones at my kennel?" "Certainly not," said Cassie Putt indignantly. "I never throw stones. It just happened to fall off as I passed by." "Happened to fall off," snorted Muffin. "A likely story. Come down here at once and explain yourself."

"No fear," thought Cassie Putt to himself. "I'm not going near that venomous little brute," although, now that he had settled down a bit, Muffin didn't really look all that fierce, and in fact he looked almost friendly as he sat scratching his stomach with one of his back feet.

"Have you got fleas?" asked Cassie Putt presently. "Fleas?" Muffin stopped scratching instantly. "Fleas?

How dare you suggest such a thing. Nasty horrible creatures. I'm only scratching because – well because it's just something dogs do."

"So," said Cassie Putt, "you haven't got fleas." He thought for a moment. "That sign above your door, *Merciless Dog* it says. I suppose that's not true either?" "Of course it's true," growled Muffin. "You just come down off that wall and I'll show you how merciless I can be. I'd have you by the throat in a trice, I would. Oh yes. I'm pretty merciless – well – a *bit* merciless." Cassie Putt looked down at him with a sorrowful expression on his face. "You're not merciless at all! It's all a front. You're as soft as butter, I can tell."

"Well," said Muffin, shuffling about a bit and chewing on a bit of a stick. "It's what humans expect you see. They think I'm a guard dog, so I do it to please them." "I shouldn't bother," sniffed Cassie Putt, "I'd please myself first." "Ah but you see, that is where dogs are different," said Muffin earnestly, "we're loyal and faithful and stuff like that, and mostly we do as we're told."

"Ah well," said Cassie Putt, "if that's how you feel, but I must say I am not all that keen on humans. There's a boy comes out into the garden sometimes. I certainly don't like *him* much. He pulled my tail once you know." "Dear oh dear," said Muffin, "you don't want to pay any heed to *that*. It's just his way of being friendly, and, I tell you, if you give him a stick, he'll throw sticks all day. Simply loves throwing sticks. Mind you it can get a bit tiring, but if you choose a time just before lunch or dinner he usually leaves off to go in and eat. You just need to know a bit about humans and I'm certain you could get to like them after a time."

Just then, a dusty grey lorry turned into the yard and a dusty grey man got out and leaned on the bonnet. Muffin got into guard dog mode instantly, barking and growling and leaping around like crazy. Soon another man came out from the house and Muffin ceased guarding and flung himself, panting, on to the ground alongside his kennel. "Tiring work, guarding," he gasped at last. "Rubbish," said Cassie Putt, "there was no need for any of that carry on at all. All you had to do was precisely nothing. The man would have heard the noise of the lorry and come out in any case. My advice is, give up the guarding and come out with me for the day." "Well of course I would like to. Very much," said Muffin, "but you see I'm attached to this chain." "Bring it along as well," cried Cassie Putt airily, springing lightly from the wall and stretching himself luxuriously in the morning sun. "But," began Muffin, "the chain, it's attached to the kennel as well, so you see, I can't really come out."

Cassie Putt was speechless for a moment. "Well now, that's exactly my point. Humans take advantage of your caring qualities. You get chained up and made to slave in the hot sun, no free time." Cassie Putt regarded Muffin for a time with a certain degree of pity. "I wish I knew how to help you. I don't do severing chains, more's the pity..." His voice trailed off. "Don't get me wrong," interrupted Muffin brightly. "I get very well fed and taken for walks and everything. I'm not really a prisoner you know."

35

"You get taken for walks," repeated Cassie Putt scathingly. "On a leash I have no doubt. Not a chance of chasing anything like a rabbit – or anything at all."

Here Cassie Putt broke off rather abruptly, as he recalled the eagerness of most dogs to chase cats as well as innocent rabbits and pretty nearly everything that had legs and ran away.

It was then that Cassie Putt realised that he was getting into deep water and dangerously close to this so-called merciless dog. Not a situation to be encouraged, so he sprang to his feet, dusted off some bits of straw and leaves, and departed abruptly towards the river and the woods.

"Is that you off then?" queried Muffin, slightly miffed at Cassie Putt's rather rushed departure. "Needs must, needs must," called Cassie Putt from the depths of a great stand of dochans, "must catch something for breakfast yet."

Muffin heaved a sigh. At least he didn't have to go out and look for his own breakfast. He riffled through his dish with "DOG" on the side, and lay down with a crunchy sort of bone. He scratched his stomach. Possibly he did have fleas.

The Green Gnome

Wimpy was a green gnome. He lived on a plastic mushroom in the centre of the front lawn, and he lived a very dull life indeed, so one day he decided to run away and be a miner. He might even find a princess recklessly abandoned in the forest.

Green gnomes, of course, always work by night, so as soon as darkness fell, off he set, with two glow-worms on a string to lead the way, down the garden path and along the avenue towards the forest.

He carried with him a stout stick with which to poke about in the undergrowth, and to ward off wild animals. The forest was certain to be teeming with tigers and lions and perhaps even a ferocious dragon.

Onward he marched into the forest. The dark trees hung low over the path, and he hoped he could find a mine quite soon, for he didn't really like the dark, and the glow-worms didn't make all that much light.

Presently, through the trees, he saw a jolly fire blazing, and as he came nearer he discovered that it was indeed a dragon, blowing long tongues of flame down his nostrils and burning up piles of dried leaves on the forest floor.

The glow-worms were terrified. They rushed off, screaming loudly, into the distance.

"Dear me," said the dragon, "I wish they would realise that dragons aren't really dangerous these days. I was only burning up these few dead leaves. Makes the forest look so untidy, leaves blowing about all over the place."

The green gnome was very relieved to find the dragon so friendly, and they talked pleasantly for a time. "Well," said the green gnome at last, "I must be off. I'm searching for a mine, you know, but they are far and few."

"How right you are," said the dragon. "I don't know what the world is coming to. I haven't seen a princess in months, never speaking of a brave knight. I'd quite enjoy a jolly good battle right now. You wouldn't like to have a quick fight before you go?" he enquired hopefully, but the green gnome backed hastily away, tucking his beard into his belt, and taking a tighter hold on his stick.

"Don't worry," said the dragon. "If you don't feel up to it, never bother. Perhaps another time?" "Yes indeed," said the green gnome, smiling in a strained manner. "Now I really must be off."

"Goodbye," called the dragon. "Good luck with the mine detecting," and he blew a scorching breath along the forest floor till the dead leaves blazed like a furnace.

The green gnome stumbled away through the bushes. It was really very dark and now that the glow-worms had deserted him he could see almost nothing.

He was just beginning to wish he had stayed at home on his plastic mushroom when, all of a sudden, down he dropped into an extremely deep hole, hitting his head a fearful blow as he fell, so that he was quite unconscious for a time.

When he opened his eyes, it was daylight, and a

princess was bending over him, patting his head with a cool cloth. All around him, picks and shovels leaned against the sides of the deep pit. He sat up at once, and the princess was most relieved to find that he had recovered.

"What sort of mine is this?" asked the green gnome eagerly. "Is it a diamond mine?" "I'm afraid it isn't a mine at all," said the princess. "It's an excavation. Roman remains, you know."

Well, of course the green gnome had never heard of the Romans, but the princess explained it all very clearly and he decided at once that this was much more interesting than mining for diamonds.

And there he is to this day, discovering bits of paving, and old coins, and singing Hey Ho almost all of the time. Much more rewarding than sitting on a plastic mushroom.

Of Mice and Many

Once upon a time, far and away across the Great Heathery Hills and over the green valleys and the shining rivers, there lived two little mice. They were very happy in their little cottage, where the pink roses cast their petals by the door, and the lawn spread velvet beneath the trees. Each day Mr Mouse set off to work, spruce and neat in his dove grey suit, with his little reticule swinging in his paw, and, after he had gone, Mrs Mouse would get out her dusters and her polish, and when she'd finished her housework, and Mr Mouse's dinner was all ready in the oven, she'd bring out her sewing and sit in the sun by the door. In summer that is, but aah…in winter…that was a different story.

Sometimes, in the morning, the snow would be piled so high along the path that poor Mr Mouse would shiver and shake as he shovelled aside the great white mounds to clear the way to work, and Mrs Mouse would cry because the pipes were frozen and her paws so cold she could hardly hold her polishing cloth. In short, Mr and Mrs Mouse hated the winter, and one day he came home from work with a great pile of holiday brochures.

"Lookee here," he cried. (Because he'd had a Chinese grandmother and he liked to keep himself in mind of her.) "I've had a wonderful idea. While all this snow and ice is around, why don't we fly off to a sunny clime?"

"Sunny clime," thought Mrs Mouse, with pictures of the Swiss Alps in mind, but Mr Mouse soon put her right on that score, and they spent the entire evening looking through all the brochures, trying to decide where to go.

"Somewhere not too hot," decided Mr Mouse, since he was inclined towards heat stroke. "And no snakes," squealed Mrs Mouse. Her favourite uncle had been swallowed by an anaconda and she didn't want to end up like *that*, thank you very much.

At last, after much cogitating, and quite a lot of thinking as well, they decided that Villa O'Ratta was the ideal spot. It even had a pool where Mrs Mouse could swim of a morning.

Such a hurrying and scurrying and packing and repacking. New sunglasses to be purchased. Lotions and creams in case of sunburn. Tablets for purifying the water. Mr Mouse even packed his favourite cheese. "You never know about those sheep milk products," he stated firmly. "They rarely look all that clean, and there's nothing like a nice bit of cheddar in any case." So it went on, until at last the day of their departure arrived. It was bitterly cold with some sleet, and Mr and Mrs Mouse stepped aboard the plane with enormous satisfaction, glad to be leaving such inclemency behind.

The Villa O'Ratta was bathed in sunshine when they arrived. Flocks of tourists filled the Strip in all sorts of gay holiday clothes. Topless, even, and Mrs Mouse was just beginning to loosen the buttons on her cardigan when Mr Mouse put his paw firmly over hers and shook his finger at her. "There are limits my love," he said quietly but firmly, and perhaps he was right.

The gardener assisted them to wheel their

baggage over the bumpy grass to their chalet, and Mr Mouse unlocked their door, and they stepped inside. The sun was streaming in through the big patio doors, and Mr Mouse flung them open and strode out onto the terrace where he stood, hands behind his back, eyes closed, revelling in the warmth of the sun. Mrs Mouse bustled about and very soon appeared with some bread and cheese on a tray, and then they both stretched themselves on their sun beds and had a little zizzz, since it had been a tiring day.

All at once, Mr Mouse heard a twig snap. Being an ex-commando and a trained Karate expert, his ears were tuned to that sort of thing. He opened one eye and froze, or rather stiffened, in fright. Stalking through the flowerbed was a gi-normous striped cat. It stopped to sniff at a flower, so Mr Mouse was able to have a jolly good look at it. It was extremely large, and no doubt dangerous. These cats always are. For some minutes the animal remained still, sniffing the flower with its eyes closed, then it lazily moved off through the bushes and disappeared. Mr Mouse slumped back on his sun bed. He glanced cautiously at Mrs Mouse, but mercifully she was still asleep and had heard nothing. This was disastrous! Cats!…But after some thought Mr Mouse decided to keep quiet about it. No sense in alarming Mrs Mouse, and who knows, the creature might never come near them again. Presently, when Mrs Mouse woke up, they both went back indoors, and Mrs Mouse made a long shopping list and they both set out to the market with a large shopping bag.

The market was wonderfully busy, and full of

all sorts of exotic stuff, so that by the time they started out for home, the shopping bag was full to overflowing with goodies and various other things that Mrs Mouse did not really need, but she thought that they would be certain to come in useful at a later date.

It took them ages to climb the long steep hill back home, and they had almost reached their door when suddenly two great black dogs erupted out of the bushes and headed straight towards them.

Mr and Mr Mouse were terrified. They squeaked and twittered and ran around in a circle and dropped their shopping and tripped over a great bank of grass by the way, and fell for miles it seemed, down into a steep gully, where they lay with their paws around each other and breathed very heavily indeed for quite a long time. Nothing happened. No dogs appeared to look over the edge, with gaping jaws and dripping fangs. All was silent. Still nothing happened, so at last they both gathered themselves together and climbed back up the bank. There was not a dog to be seen. They'd gone, and, wonder of wonders, their bag of shopping still lay where it had fallen. To be sure, they lost no time in picking it up, and with their hearts in their mouths they scampered back to their chalet, unlocked the door and tumbled quickly inside.

That night it was a long time before they got to sleep, but at last Mrs Mouse dropped off. As soon as he was certain she was asleep, Mr Mouse climbed out of bed and slipped quietly downstairs to the bathroom where he spent quite a long time polishing up on all his most effective Karate moves, finishing with his speciality, a series of lightning chops and an extremely high kick. He put such an effort into this last move that he almost did himself a mischief, but it did wonders for his confidence, and after that he felt sure he could cope with anything that might crop up, and, returning to his bed, he slept heavily till morning.

And it was the morning that brought the final and worst blow of all. Mr Mouse had just finished cutting himself a particularly fine piece of cheese and was arranging it alongside his crisp bread when the noise of an arrival outside the door caught his attention. Loud voices, the rattle of trolley wheels, and finally, the sound of a key turning in the door. Mr Mouse clutched the arms of his chair, his eyes riveted on the now opening door. He could hardly believe it. Four giants stood on the steps, and, even as he caught Mrs Mouse's paw in his and ran for the stairs, they all marched purposefully into the chalet, dropping their goods and chattels on every available surface. Mr and Mrs Mouse sprang into the wardrobe and slammed the door.

They were breathing heavily *again*. There was a space at the bottom of the wardrobe door and, after a time, the two mice lay down on their stomachs and peered out through the space into the room. No doubt about it, the giants intended to stay. They were unpacking, making coffee, running the shower…one was already asleep on the bed, and beginning to snore very loudly. The mice were aghast! What to do? They could stay in the wardrobe of course, but what about food?

One of the giants left a large crust by the bedside,

44

and that night Mr Mouse girded his loins and sallied forth to capture the crust, and, after a deal of bother managed to hoist it up into the wardrobe. They feasted on that for some days, but soon every crumb was eaten, and they began to feel very hungry indeed.

At last, after the mice had waited for days, all four giants went out together, and Mr and Mrs Mouse crept from their hiding place and began to stuff themselves with whatever scraps they could find.

They were so busy eating they never even *heard* the giants returning, and they were caught red-handed in the middle of the floor. Such a screaming and a shouting, and a leaping onto beds and a wringing of hands. Suddenly, the mice found themselves in the bedroom. One of the giants slammed the door with a thunderous crash, and they were prisoners, alone in the dark. What a circumstance! The mice were terrified. They could hear the giants muttering and planning in the next room. Eventually, all was quiet, and the two mice crept across the floor and peered through the crack in the woodwork. All four giants were asleep, head to toe, all together in one bed, which is what giants do when they are planning something absolutely diabolical, and is a *very bad sign*.

Mr Mouse pulled himself firmly together. Something must be done, and *fast*. He made a careful reconnaissance of the room. Of course! The ventilator! With great difficulty he at last managed to lever himself up and after much whimpering and falling backwards onto the floor, Mrs Mouse was encouraged to climb up beside him. They scrambled out through the grille into the garden and at last they were free.

"Well that's it!" said Mr Mouse decisively, brushing the dust off his Bermuda shorts. "That's it! We're going *home*. It's cold, it's wet, it's damp and it's dull, but at least it's safe."

They both picked up their tails and ran, swift as the wings of the humming bird, into The Great Wide Yonder.

One Good Turn

Once upon a time there was a rabbit – an ordinary rabbit with a grey furry coat and a white stripe down his nose, but he was just a little bit different. He had no name. All the other rabbits had names like Bobtail and Flop-ears and Dylan. There was one called Cheese as well – he was a welsh rabbit. There was even one called Jan Van Der Bun, who had been named after a Dutch uncle in the family.

Well then, when this rabbit was born, his mother seemed to have run out of names, or perhaps she was too busy to think of one, or maybe she just never got around to choosing one. Anyhow, there he was without a name and beginning to get very tired of being called Jock or Fred or Mush, or even just "hey you!"

One day, when he was lolloping slowly past the palace and thinking of nothing in particular, he became aware of a great deal of banging and shouting, and the sound of doors slamming. A slipper flew out of an upstairs window, followed almost immediately by a hairbrush, all signs of someone in a great rage. The grey rabbit guessed at once that it must be the Princess. No one else would be allowed to carry on in such a disgraceful manner.

At that moment, a footman appeared at the side gate looking anxiously up the road in the direction of the town. The grey rabbit stopped to ask the reason for all the noise, and the footman explained that the Princess had lost her powder puff and although the palace had been searched from top to bottom not a trace of it could be found. A messenger had been dispatched to town to buy a new one, but had not yet returned, and the Princess was in a great tantrum at the delay.

Soon a cloud of dust appeared in the distance and as it grew nearer the grey rabbit discerned the King's messenger galloping his horse furiously back to the palace with the dread news that not a powder puff could be bought in town. What was to be done? In her present temper, the Princess was quite likely to have them clapped in irons for a month or even longer when she discovered they still hadn't got a powder puff for her.

All of a sudden the grey rabbit had a bright idea. He'd managed not too badly without a name, perhaps he'd get along just as well without a tail. Quickly he tied one end of a length of string to his tail and the other end he fixed securely to the handle of the palace door. Then he rang the bell loudly.

Soon footsteps approached down the long corridor and the butler pulled the door open. There was a sharp tug and off flew the grey rabbit's tail on the end of the piece of string. Picking it up, he dusted it carefully on his sleeve, and, bowing low, he presented it with his compliments to the Princess, who came down the stairs at that moment.

Everyone was delighted and the King sent for the grey rabbit at once and ordered him to wait while he had a quick rummage through his desk to find his list of ministers. This was soon found and the King selected a suitable title for the grey rabbit, which he conferred upon him on the instant along with various other gifts. Now, when the grey rabbit goes walking, everyone stands aside with raised hats and says, "Ah! There goes the Minister Without."

Calamity

Once upon a time, there was a cloud of peedie black flies, singing in the sun, and one day they decided to set out and see the world. So, off they went, all ten.

"What a wonderful world," cried the first peedie fly, buzzing down to admire his reflection in the lily pond, when down he fell into the water, and that was the end of him.

"Calamity!" cried the flies. "That's what comes of being vain," and they flew on till they came to a garden full of flowers. "This is all for me," cried the second peedie fly, but a bird swooped by and gobbled him up, and that was the end of him.

"Calamity!" cried the flies. "That's what comes of being selfish," and they flew on till they came to the sea. "Listen to the song of the sea," cried the third peedie fly, standing with his back to the ocean; and a huge wave came and washed him away, and that was the end of him.

"Calamity!" cried the flies. "That's what comes of being careless," and they flew on till they came to a honey-pot. "Hurrah!" cried the fourth peedie fly. "I shall eat till I burst," so he did, and that was the end of him.

"Calamity!" cried the flies. "That's what comes of being greedy", and they flew on till they came to a candle burning brightly. "Keep away!" cried the flies but the fifth peedie fly went too near and singed his wings, and that was the end of him.

"Calamity!" cried the flies. "That's what comes

of being disobedient," and they flew on till they came to a railway line. "Let's stay for a while," cried the sixth peedie fly, but a train came by, and that was the end of him.

"Calamity!" cried the flies. "That's what comes of dawdling," and they flew on till they came to a long sticky flypaper. "What can this be?" wondered the seventh peedie fly, and sat down to think, and that was the end of him.

"Calamity!" cried the flies. "That's what comes of being inquisitive," and they flew on till they came to a green frog sitting on a stone. "A very good morning to you," cried the eighth peedie fly, and the green frog shot out his tongue and gobbled him up, and that was the end of him.

"Calamity!" cried the flies. "That's what comes of speaking to strangers," and they flew on till they came to a glittering spider's web. "I must go in," cried the ninth peedie fly, and that was the end of him.

"Calamity!" cried the last peedie fly. "That's what comes of being foolish," and he flew on for miles till he lost his way, and that was the end of him.

The Fire Dragon

Once upon a time, far and away across the Great
Heathery Hill, in the land of the Orcs, there lived a
fearsome Hilly Trow.

In a deep dark cave beneath the rocks, here he
dwelt, with a great green mound around the entrance,
which was so small that only a rat could pass through,
because, of course, Hilly Trows are marvellously magical
and can shrink themselves small as small.

In the croft lands round and about the people
lived in fear and trembling for they never knew when
the wicked Hilly Trow would come down through the
grey rocks to plunder and steal and cast his evil eye on
anyone who crossed his path.

Then one day, when the corn lay gold in the
valley, and the crofters were labouring with heuk and
sickle to harvest the grain, the wicked Hilly Trow crept
from his lair and stole a precious baby that lay asleep
among the sheaves.

Such a weeping and a wailing there was, but
though they cried and pleaded, the cruel Hilly Trow
carried the baby away, and it was never seen again.

As time went by, the poor crofters became more
and more afraid and at last they decided to move far
away from the haunts of the Hilly Trow, so they left their
fine pasture land to dwell by the stony shore where they
lived on rainbow fish from the sea and shell creatures
from the rock pools.

Here they stayed for many a day till by chance

a longship came by carrying fierce men from the Far North Land, and the crofters welcomed the strangers and entertained them with much feasting and song. Then their eyes grew dim and their voices sad as they told the strangers of the wicked Hilly Trow and his evil ways, and how they had fled from their fine crofts to escape from him.

The men from the Far North Land harkened to the tale for they too had wild Trolls who dwelt in the high hills of home, and together they made a plan to defeat the wicked monster.

They resolved to build a great fire at the entrance to the cave, for Hilly Trows, like all wild and wicked creatures, are afraid of fire. They would build a fire like no other fire. A fire that would never die. And there it is to this day, carved in stone upon the inner wall, a fiery dragon breathing fire that only a Hilly Trow can see, and fear. And may it so remain, forever, and always.

All for One

The kettle had been newly polished and was admiring his reflection in the shiny enamel of the stove back. "What a splendid looking fellow I am," he said aloud, blowing a cloud of steam from his spout. "I should not be surprised if I were the best looking kettle in the whole world, and easily the most useful person in the kitchen. What would everybody do without me? There would be no cups of tea or hot drinks or even a spot of boiling water for the potatoes. I really am a very important kettle."

He blew out another cloud of steam and was just about to burst into song when a dirty black poker, all covered with soot and bits of melted coal, clattered onto the stove top and fell carelessly against the kettle, leaving a dirty sooty mark along his shining side.

The kettle was furious. "How dare you come barging up here," he cried. "Look what you've done, you careless lout! You should show some respect for your betters!"

"My betters!" exclaimed the poker. "You've got to be joking. There you sit idly admiring yourself while I struggle about doing all the very dirty work, clearing the ashes and breaking up the coal. You wouldn't get on very well without me, I can tell you. I'm the king pin around here and no mistake."

The kettle flipped his lid in a great rage, but while he was spluttering and hissing trying to think of something very crushing to say, a third voice piped

53

up. It was the kettle holder hanging from a hook close by. "You really are a stupid pair," said the kettle holder. "Where would you be without me? I'm the one who's brought in when things get too hot to handle! I'm the one everybody looks for. I'm the one! I'm the one!"

At that moment there was a great roar from the fire, and the door of the stove burst open. "Be silent all of you!" blazed the fire. I'm sick of all your boasting and arguments. Where do you think you'd all be if it weren't for me down here? You'd be quite useless, that's what you'd be, so stop your silly quarrelling and let's have some peace and quiet around here!" So saying, he puffed a cloud of smoke into the room and closed the fire door with a bang.

There was not a sound for quite some time; then the kettle heaved a big sigh and began to sing softly. "One might as well keep cheerful in any event," he said thoughtfully to himself.

Hare-on-the-Hill

Hare-on-the-Hill was asleep, curled in a tight brown ball in his shallow form beneath the gorse bushes.

Presently it began to snow, and the powdery flakes swirled through the spiky branches of the bushes and sifted in around the roots, and when evening came, only the tip-most tops of the branches could be seen.

Hare-on-the-Hill opened his yellow eyes and stretched his long legs into the snow all around him, then he scrambled quickly through the drift and bounded forth into the bright moonshine.

Down over the sloping fields the snow did not lie so deeply, and Hare-on-the-Hill found plenty to eat by way of turnip tops and kale, and when he had eaten his fill, he danced madly over the icy meadows, flinging the snow on every side. Soon he grew tired of this sport, and, just as dawn came up in the sky, he crawled once more into his form to sleep.

Curiously enough, it was delightfully warm in his snowy bed, and as the days went by he began to wish he could stay there forever. But soon a change came in on the wind, the sky grew cold like steel and it began to rain.

When morning came the fields lay dark and sodden, with only a drift of dingy white under the lee, and melting snow ran by the way in a dirty stream.

Hare-on-the-Hill stirred in his cold wet bed. How he longed for the warmth of his snow house. After a time, he began to think of his friend the rabbit, warm all year round in his deep burrow, and he decided to dig for himself just such a shelter. He set to with a will, scattering the wet earth behind him as he dug, and soon he had made a deep tunnel in the hillside with a gentle hollow at the end for his bed.

But as the days passed a great deal of water seeped down into the tunnel, and he became cold and cramped. There was little room to stretch his long legs. It did not feel at all like his snow house. It was damp and dark, and the smell of the wet earth choked him. He was glad when night came and he could escape over the darkening fields, bounding free as the wind, where the air was fresh and clear, with rain drifting away over the hill, and the stars swinging bright in the north.

Hare-on-the-Hill sat once more beneath the gorse bushes. A little drying wind had sprung up and there was a hint of spring in the air. He scratched the black tip of one long ear and riffled through the withered grass in his old form, then curled himself into a tight brown ball and went to sleep. Morning was at hand, and the clouds to the east had a rim of gold.

The Treasure Box

Once upon a time, in the long gone days, the Great
Muckle Grullyan was eltan in the ebb when he came
upon a large iron-bound box washed up on the shore.
It was firmly closed and black with age, and covered
in barnacles and long streamers of green seaweed, and
when the Muckle Grullyan tried to lift it he could move
it only the slightest little bit as it was so heavy.

"Aha," thought the Muckle Grullyan to himself,
"I have found a treasure. Surely this box must be full
of gold, or silver at the very least, to be so heavy?" He
looked all around to see if anyone had seen him find
the box, but no one was in sight so he decided to hide it
till it was dark, and then come back for it, for if anyone
should see him, as sure as sure they'd come offering to
help him carry it and then, as like as not, they'd want a
share of the treasure. He covered it over carefully with
seaweed and marked the spot with a stone, then made
off home till it was dark.

Surely that day dragged by. Never had the
sun stayed so long in the sky. Never had there been
such cloudless weather, so that not a beam of light
was wasted. The Muckle Grullyan was in a fever of
impatience for the darkness to fall, but at last the sun
began to sink, the golden sky grew dim, and soon the
dark velvet night had come.

The Muckle Grullyan wrapped himself in his
great cloak, picked up his heavy staff and crept out into
the dark night. Not a one did he see as he slipped along,

and soon he came to the stony shore and began to look for the spot where he had hidden the iron-bound box.

He looked and he looked, this way and that, becoming more and more alarmed as he began to think he had hidden the box too well, but there at last was the stone marking the spot, and there was the box still hidden under the seaweed.

He dragged away the slimy weed and began to consider what would be the best way to shift the box. It was much too heavy to lift and carry, so finally he decided he'd move it end over end up the beach, and he set to work at once.

Such a noise he made, thundering over the rocks and chingle with the great box, so it was not surprising that someone should hear him. First of all, an old grey limpet came trolling up on his one flat foot.

"Ho there Muckle Grullyan," cried the limpet. "Can I be of some assistance?" "Get away and mind your own business," growled the Muckle Grullyan, still heaving and pushing at the great box, and beginning to feel quite exhausted.

Soon two or three more limpets came on the scene and very shortly there were rows of peedie buckies and hermit crabs and the like, all pushing and jostling each other in the moonlight to get a better view. The Muckle Grullyan was furious.

"Get away home," he shouted. "You're getting none of my treasure," but of course no one paid any heed.

At last the Muckle Grullyan reached the top of the shore and leaned against a large stone whilst he rested for a moment, but by some dreadful mischance the box slipped and it rolled down the beach once more, where it burst open with a loud crash.

With all speed, the Muckle Grullyan clambered back down after it, expecting to see the treasure spread among the chingle, but not a treasure was there. The great box had been empty all the time. Not a single thing was in it.

How the peedie limpets laughed. They laughed and they laughed and they laughed. They fell about on their sides with laughing, and the Muckle selfish old Grullyan made off into the darkness in a black rage. Which only goes to show that it doesn't pay to be greedy.

The Bouncing Ball

Once upon a time there was a blue bouncing ball. Every day he was out in the garden, bouncing up and down the wide path, sometimes low and sometimes high.

Sometimes he'd bounce just as high as the tall pink foxgloves so that he could see right down into their spotted faces, and sometimes he'd bounce high, high, till he could see far and away over the garden wall, to where the man next door dug and planted in his flower beds and where the red geraniums glowed like fire through the windows of the glass house. Once he even bounced as high as the roof but that was not so nice, because he almost got stuck in the narrow guttering, and the blue ball was very glad when he bounced back down on to the smooth path, and he rolled quickly away into the shade of the lupins to recover.

One day the blue bouncing ball was enjoying a fine game of cricket, skimming over the grass like an arrow and cracking down on the bat like a bullet, when a dreadful thing happened. He misjudged the distance over the grass, crashed through the fuchsia hedge and hit the wall at the other side with a mighty thump. Down he fell quite dazed into the shallow drain, and, before he could stop himself, he rolled slowly through the broken grating at the end and dropped into the water below.

So dark it was down that drain, and the water was full of bits of stick and dead leaves and green horrible slime. The blue bouncing ball was very distressed and bobbed about through the rubbish looking for a way out, but there was none, and he gazed sadly up at the high grating through which he had fallen and which was now far out of reach.

At last he spied a small opening in the side of his prison and floated across to it. Perhaps if he squeezed himself very small he might manage to escape through it? He scrunched himself up till he was small as he could be and squeezed into the hole. And there the blue bouncing ball stuck fast. He wriggled and shoved and pushed and twisted, but not a fraction could he budge. He was a captive in the deep dark drain.

Up above in the bright garden, they looked and they looked this way and that for the blue bouncing ball. The long shadows fell across the green lawn and the day grew chill. Soon they gave up the search and the garden was quiet and still and empty.

Large black clouds crowding in from the bay filled the sky, and great fat drops of rain began to fall, bouncing off the pavements and rushing down the gutters and the drains. Water came flooding through the grating into the dark drain where the blue bouncing ball was still imprisoned, but there was no way out for the water because there was the blue bouncing ball blocking the way out, so the drain filled up and the water overflowed all over the path, making a fearful puddle.

Someone came and poked about in the drain with a stick but to no avail; and the lid had to be prised up and all the bits of rubbish had to be sifted out, and here they found the blue bouncing ball wedged in the drainpipe. He was lifted carefully out, and away he bounded up the path, peering over the wall at the man next door, and bouncing over the tall spotted foxgloves.

An Odd Fellow

Once upon a time there was a grey rabbit. Each day at the crack of dawn he'd spring up from his burrow and sit on the sand at the entrance to sniff the fresh dewy smell of the morning.

Surely it was the best time of the day, with the mist lifting and melting away in the first beams of the sun, and the perfume of mint and clover beginning to drift over the grass.

One morning the grey rabbit sprang up as usual and sat on the sand gulping in great breaths of the fresh morning air. Just for a minute he thought he smelt something unusual, but it was gone again like a flash. Next morning a stiff breeze blew, and all the morning smells were swept out to sea; so the grey rabbit spent no time sniffing the air. But on the third morning there was only a light breath of wind, and the grey rabbit could quite distinctly smell something not very nice at all. He looked around this way and that, and there, almost hidden in a clump of dusty nettles, lay a sordid little heap of black feathers. It was a dead corbie.

The grey rabbit backed off in distaste. What a perfect nuisance. He would have to get rid of the dead bird at once; but he didn't fancy having to do the job himself. Just then a brilliant red admiral flitted into view and perched among the nettles, opening and closing his velvet wings in the sunshine.

"Do you see that bird?" asked the grey rabbit. "How about giving me a hand to remove it? The smell is becoming quite strong, and it's most inconvenient, almost on my doorstep." The red admiral flew up in horror. "Certainly not! I wouldn't dream of touching it." And he vanished abruptly into the distance.

"Now isn't that just typical of those flighty creatures," said the grey rabbit to himself. "Not a thought for anyone but themselves. Surely someone will help me get rid of this nuisance?" He sat up, shading his eyes and looking hopefully around. After a time he saw a kirsty kringlick approaching unsteadily over the tall grass, dipping and swerving and getting his long legs entangled every so often as he drew near.

"Help!" shouted the grey rabbit. "Come here. I need your help." But the kirsty kringlick paid no heed to his cries, and blundered away through the grasses, looking this way and that with his dull grey eyes, and disappearing slowly over the rim of the hill.

"What a very stupid fellow," grumbled the grey rabbit. "I'm positive he didn't hear me on purpose." Not that one could blame the kirsty kringlick. After all, not too many people wish to become involved in such an unpleasant task.

The grey rabbit once more sat down sadly on the grass, trying not to look in the direction of the dead bird. Something would have to be done about it, and as no help was forthcoming, he would have to do the job himself. He climbed slowly to his feet, but just at that moment there was a sharp clatter of wings and a big sexton beetle landed clumsily beside him on the sand.

"Ho there!" said the beetle, noisily closing his wings and folding them away neatly on his back. "You

64

look rather worried."
"Indeed I am," said the grey
rabbit. "Take a look over there."
"I say," said the beetle, hurrying
over to the corbie and poking
at it with his feelers.
"What a perfectly splendid
dead bird. How did you come
by it? I've been on the lookout
for just such a one for some days,
but without any luck. May I give
you a hand to bury it?"

The grey rabbit was quite speechless. "Why – er
– certainly," he said. "Perhaps," went on the beetle, "if I
help you, you might even see your way to giving me a
tiny share, by way of reward." "A tiny share?" said the
grey rabbit. "You can have the whole lot if you wish.
What on earth would I do with a dead bird? All I want
is to get it out of the way and be rid of that dreadful
smell."

The sexton beetle was amazed. Here he had been
searching for just such a prize for days, and this foolish
rabbit was throwing it carelessly away. Certainly there
were some funny people about, he thought to himself, as
he started digging with a will.

Seeing the beetle so busily employed the grey
rabbit slipped quietly away. If that stupid beetle was so
keen, he was welcome to do all the work himself. And
as he nibbled at a frond of fresh grass, the grey rabbit
said to himself: "What an odd fellow! What a *very* odd
fellow!"

The Eel Well

Once upon a time, close by the old wall at the foot of the brae, in the peedie park where the dochans spread their rusty leaves in the damp shade, there was a well. Its steep sides were built of stone, and over the top there lay a great stone slab. Three stone steps led down inside to where the sweet spring water bubbled up in the cool dark, and here in the deepermost corner of the deep dark well there lived a brown eel.

Each year, the eel was captured in a bucket, while the weeds and slime were scrubbed from the stone sides of the well and the muddy water emptied far out on the grassy banks, leaving the well once more sweet and clean. Then the eel would be tipped gently back in, to hide in a cranny till the spring water crept up again to the level of the lower step, and the brown eel had room to glide and quiver in the deepening water.

As time went on he began to grow tired of his cramped life in the deep dark well and longed to escape, but the sides of his prison were too steep and rough.

At length the spring came again and once more the brown eel was lifted out of the water to wait in the bucket while the well was cleaned. The children came round and peered in at him and he looked back at them with his stony little eyes and wound himself slowly round and round. Then somehow there was a scuffle, the bucket was tipped over and the big brown eel vanished into the deep grass. He slithered through the thick red stems of the dochans and squeezed through a gap in the stone wall to where the gowans grew yellow on the banks of the loch and the king cups shone in the segs. The muddy water closed over him and he swam and he swam. He was free.

For many days he explored his shining new world, swimming through the shallows where the sun shone down into the sandy pools, and gliding under the bridge to where the reeds grew thick along the bank of the loch. Here the coots and water hens built their floating nests and the wild swan sat on her four white eggs. Here the ducks muttered on the pebbled shore and the black cattle drowsed knee deep in the water.

The big brown eel had never been so happy, and he grew bold and fearless, swimming far and away to the very furthest corner of the shining loch. There he began to feel a different movement in the water. A chill began to creep into the world and he felt himself carried gently along, slowly at first and then faster and faster till he was swept into the wide mouth of a deep drain and borne swiftly into the darkness.

The big brown eel was very frightened, but the water was flowing too strongly for him to turn back, and soon he was carried far out into the wide green sea. The water was cold and bitter, and the big brown eel began to wish he had never left his safe home in the deep dark well. The wild waves dashed him roughly against the sharp rocks till at last he found shelter under a sloping canopy of seaweed, and here he lay, thinking sadly that he would never see his home again.

Soon he heard a snuffling and a scratching among the rocks, and he grew stiff with horror and fright. A sleek otter was hunting for food nearby, and the big brown eel lay like a stone with never a movement till the otter passed slowly by, looking and searching. Then at last he was gone, and the big brown eel was safe.

After a time, he ventured out of his hiding place and began to search for the way back to the loch, and soon he found the spot. The water still flowed down, but not so strongly as before, and the big brown eel battled slowly up through the dark drain, till he came again to the still waters of the loch.

He rested gladly in the dappled shallows, watching the fat red water beetles hunting busily in the drifting lilies. The water was warm and smooth as silk and the big brown eel basked lazily in a patch of yellow sunshine that gleamed down through the weeds. Suddenly a grey shadow drifted across the water and a pair of sharp red eyes spied the big brown eel. In an instant the heron caught him in his cruel beak and carried him swiftly away across the loch.

The big brown eel squirmed and wriggled and wound himself round and round, trying desperately to escape, till at last the heron was forced to drop him, and down he fell, screaming silently through the still air, till he fell among the broad leaves of the dochans that grew round the old well, and slid like a shining brown ribbon down into the deepermost corner of the deep dark well.

The Silver Bridle

Once upon a time, in the long gone days, the Muckle Grullyan went to the mart, and when he was poking and prying among the goods what should he come upon but a splendid saddle and bridle, in smooth supple leather, with silver buckles and hung about with silver ornaments.

He made up his mind at once to buy them for his great black horse, and his delight knew no bounds when the bridle was his. He held it up to admire it, turning it this way and that, polishing the buckles on his sleeve, and running his fingers over the smooth leather. Alas, he spent so long gloating over his prize that when he turned round to buy the saddle to go with it, he discovered, to his chagrin, that a Nokh, who lived over the Great Heathery Hill, had already bought it and carried it off.

The Muckle Grullyan was furious, and went home muttering darkly to himself, and wondering how he could lay his hands on the splendid saddle.

Next morning, while the Muckle Grullyan was supping a great bowl of leaped gibbo, what should he hear but a Nokh at the door. "Ho there, Muckle Grullyan!" cried the Nokh. "May I borrow your fine silver bridle for my horse to wear, along with his splendid leather saddle, to the Horse Show?" The Muckle Grullyan was so angry that for a moment he could not think of a suitably crushing refusal. Then he realised that if he humoured the Nokh it might be to his own advantage later on, so he agreed to lend the bridle. He wrapped it carefully in a piece of sacking and the Nokh departed on his horse after promising to return the bridle without fail, in the evening.

That afternoon, as was his wont, the Muckle Grullyan went down to the singing sand and walked by the brink of the sounding sea, and as he walked he plotted and planned how he might obtain the fine leather saddle.

At last he hit upon a treacherous scheme. When the Nokh returned the bridle in the evening, he would invite him in for supper, and while the Nokh was eating, the Muckle Grullyan meant to slip outside on some pretext and exchange the fine leather saddle for an old one. When he left in the darkness, the Nokh would never notice that it was not his own fine leather saddle.

Well pleased with his plan, the Muckle Grullyan turned towards home, hugging himself with delight and every so often giving a little skip into the air as he thought of the evening.

At last, just in the grimplins, the Muckle Grullyan heard the ring of hooves on the stony brae, and the Nokh rode up on his horse. He carried the bridle carefully wrapped and the Muckle Grullyan took it hastily and placed it in a corner, smiling like a crocodile the while. The Nokh was not that anxious to come in for supper, but at last he allowed his horse to be tied to the iron ring at the end of the house, while he waited for the Muckle Grullyan to pour out a mug of blatho and spread a smear of butter on an oatcake.

No sooner had the Nokh sat down at the table

than the Muckle Grullyan made an excuse to go outside, and with all speed he exchanged his old saddle for the one on the Nokh's horse, finding the task quite difficult in the darkness. At last it was done and when he went back into the house, he found the Nokh impatient to be off, so he bade him an eager goodbye.

Almost before the sound of horses' hooves had faded in the distance, the Muckle Grullyan hurried outside for the saddle, dragging it gleefully back into the light, but alas it was not the fine leather saddle he had expected to see but an old broken one hardly holding together. Then a dreadful thought struck him. He lifted up the bridle still wrapped in the sacking, hardly daring to open it. When he did, his worst fears were realised. It was not the lovely silver bridle but a battered companion to the saddle lying at his feet. The Nokh had beaten him at his own game. Which only goes to show that loans never come laughing home

None for the Pot

Once upon a time there was a white drake. In a long
gone spring he had been a yellow duckling, running
busily through the wet grass in the morning, with
hunched shoulders and bent head, dredging titbits from
the dew, and sometimes standing on tiptoe with his
stubby wings outstretched, to capture a passing insect.

Every scrap of food that came within his reach
was shovelled down his greedy neck, and soon he was
no longer a yellow duckling but a big white drake with a
curling feather in his tail, and a voice like a pedlar.

Then, one day, the farmer's wife came out to catch
a bird for the market, and, being the largest and noisiest,
the white drake was the first to take her eye, and next
thing he knew he had been firmly laid hold of and
imprisoned in a cardboard box. In a flurry of feathers
and string he was carried off he knew not where.

Later, in the noisy market place, after much
haggling and shouting, he was sold to a man who took
him home, still in the cardboard box tied with string.
He was placed on the kitchen floor with the lid opened,
and a circle of faces peered in at the white drake. There
was a great deal of talk concerning things like roasting
and brown gravy, with orange sauce and green peas
and the white drake put his head on the side and looked
anxiously from one face to the other. But two faces had
eyes with tears, and after a time he was let loose in a
dark shed full of potatoes and boxes and the like, with a
dish of water and some grain in a flat tin. In a day or two

the door was opened and the white drake was allowed to go outside into the rain and the green grass, where he stretched his neck and flapped his wings in the wind.

But he was lonely all by himself in the garden and kept looking for a way out so that he could join his brothers and sisters in the far meadow. All day he waddled sadly up and down, peering hopefully among the bushes, but not a friend could he find.

Some time later, after the white drake had almost given up hope of finding anyone to keep him company, a Hessian bag was emptied on the grass and out tumbled the most elegant little brown duck anyone could wish to see. She had a white ring round her neck and a black feather in each wing tip.

They flew across the grass to greet one another, nodding and cawing and muttering in pleased surprise and then they set out side by side waddling contentedly round the garden, shovelling up slugs and insects for titbits.

And perhaps in a new spring there will be a nest of green eggs in the shelter of the rhubarb leaves? You never can tell.

Coral Creechurs

Once upon a time, far and away down in the deeps of the deep dark ocean, lived the Creechurs. So far and so deep they lived that even the sun could not reach that far, and so dark and so dim that some of the fishes had tiny lanterns hung above their heads to help them find the way.

The Creechurs were so tiny that they could hardly be seen, and their very favourite task was building. All day long they were busy, sifting through the warm sea water collecting grains to build their tiny houses, all heaped one upon the other, till they grew into great banks of coral along the sea bed.

Although they were so small, there were so many of them that their buildings grew surprisingly quickly, and one day they decided to build the highest building in the whole wide sea.

Out along the dim seabed the great foundations spread and up through the dark sea into the light grew the towering pillars, till at length they reached above the crested waves and it was an island, with warm tropical seas swirling round the brim.

By and by a floating branch wedged itself firmly among the sharp coral. Bits of weed and flotsam became entangled in their turn and each and every day the winds and tides brought some more. Wandering sea birds, dipping and gliding over the waves, carried grasses and seeds from the far lands, to grow and spread their clinging roots and green leaves over the bleaching coral. And still beneath the heaving ocean, the tiny Creechurs built and plastered forming great caves and caverns, where the sea swirled and sighed, and where a mighty throng of the strange creatures of the deep made their dwellings. On this ever widening foundation, the coral grew and spread till it had formed a circular reef with a quiet lagoon in the centre.

Man came and built a shelter, swam and fished in the tide pools, and lay in the cool shade of the growing trees, eating the ripe fruit and berries and listening to the brilliant birds swinging and singing in the sunny branches.

Such things grow from the least of beginnings.

The Large Brown Mouse

Once upon a time there lived a very large dark brown mouse. Besides being large, he was also quite disgustingly fat, and the reason he was so fat was simply because he ate far too much. First thing in the morning he would be rattling about in the bread bin, and getting the frying pan on the stove, and nibbling bits off the egg while the bacon was frying, and brewing up great pots of tea and toasting mounds of bread, and thinking all the while about what he would have for lunch and tea.

When he went out to do the shopping his pockets would be bulging with crisps and chocolate and peanuts, to ward off the pangs of hunger till he got home again, so it was little wonder that he grew fatter and fatter. His friends became quite ashamed of him, and once when he decided it was time he got himself a wife to look after him, all the lady mice whom he approached only laughed and said they didn't want to spend the rest of their lives slaving over a hot stove cooking for a great fat mouse like him.

One day, as he was ambling slowly past the pantry door, he noticed that it had been left carelessly open, and such a delicious smell of food wafted through that he could not resist it, and when he peeped round the door, there were shelves laden with all sorts of scrumptious things – cream cakes and butter sponges and meringues and the like. The prospect was so inviting that he just had to go in, although he knew that if the kitchen cat spied him he would not stand much chance in a race.

Such a feast the large brown mouse had! He nibbled bits of this and that, and rather more than he should of a rich fruitcake. At last he became so full that he could hardly move, and he began to feel quite sleepy, so he leaned up against a large blue honey jar and fell fast asleep. He slept so soundly that he never heard the maid come in and go out again, shutting the door sharply behind her, and when he woke up some time later, he discovered that he was firmly closed in. He was not too worried, however, with such a plentiful supply of food ready to hand, so he sat down happily by a large plate of cheese and ate contentedly while he waited for the door to be opened once more.

But time went by and no one came, and it began to grow dark, and still no one came; so the large brown mouse resigned himself to being shut all night in the pantry, and after quite a hearty supper of mince pie he settled down once more against the honey jar.

Morning came at last, and when the large brown mouse woke up and looked around he found he was still a prisoner, and oddly enough he didn't feel much like having any breakfast. The sight of so much rich food so early in the morning quite ruined his appetite, and he began to wish he had never come into the pantry in the first place. By this time he was beginning to feel dreadfully thirsty, and wished for nothing so much as a glass of clear water, but it seemed there was everything in this pantry but the one thing he craved for.

No one came near the pantry all day, because although the large brown mouse didn't know this, the

Master and Mistress had gone out for the weekend, so that by the time they came back home, the large brown mouse was almost mad with thirst.

However, all things come to an end, and when at last the Master and Mistress came home and the maid opened the pantry door to get something for supper, the large brown mouse was out in a flash and away down the corridor as fast as he could go. As soon as he got home he drank down two glasses of water one after the other and then sat down in his chair and sipped a third one.

"What a nasty experience," he thought. "Never will I put so much as a whisker round that pantry door again." And do you know, from that day to this, he has never even looked at a cream bun or a fruitcake. In fact, he has quite gone off rich food and can hardly be persuaded to have a second cup of tea.

Which only goes to show you can have a great deal too much of a good thing.

The Keelieworm

Once upon a time there was a keelieworm. She lived
on a large green cabbage, and each day, from dawn till
dusk, she spent every single moment eating and eating.
One morning she woke up feeling rather out of sorts.

In fact the more she thought about it the more out
of sorts she felt, and she had just decided that she might
as well go back to bed for a little longer, when she heard
a rustling in the tall grasses nearby, and a glossy black
slug slid into view.

"Good morning, dearie," cried the slug. "You're
up and about early!" "Yes indeed," replied the
keelieworm. "Up and about to go back to bed again. I
feel almost ill." "You do have a nasty colour," said the
slug, "and if I may say so, you seem to have let your
appearance go a bit. You look quite old and wrinkled.
It's all that lying about roasting in the sun on those
cabbage leaves. Dries up the skin. I *never* go out in the
hot sun and look at *my* lovely dewy complexion. Get
some vitamin tablets and a jar of moisturising cream.
You'll feel like a new worm… Well, I must be off, dearie
- the sun is coming up." And so saying, the slug hoisted
a frilly sunshade to ward off the first pale sunshine, and
slid off up the path, leaving a silvery trail behind her in
the dew.

The keelieworm felt even more depressed than
before, and began to wander slowly down the path,
thinking that a walk might do her good. After a time
she heard someone singing, and when she came round

a bend in the path what should she see but a glittering dark brown forky-tail stretched seductively on a leaf. She was wearing a tight cocktail dress and was busy polishing her nails. The keelieworm felt sorrier for herself than ever when she saw this elegant creature, although she did think the dress was hardly suitable for that early hour.

"Hi darling," crooned the forky-tail, waving her hands about in the air to dry the polish. "It's not all go with you this morning, I can see." "It certainly is not," agreed the keelieworm, settling down against a pebble to take the weight off her feet. "I need pepping up a bit. Do you think perhaps a new hair-do might help?"

"Well," began the forky-tail rather doubtfully, "you could try a colour rinse I suppose, but actually darling, don't you think you've left it just a teensy weensy bit too late? I mean to say..." and the ill-mannered creature actually laughed.

The poor keelieworm felt herself burning up with shame and indignation. How dare that vulgar creature make a fool of her. She got to her feet as quickly as she could and hurried off.

Farther on down the stone path she spied a jumping jeck on a flat stone. He was dressed in a singlet and shorts and was lying on his back doing cycling exercises in the air, but when he saw the keelieworm he sprang to his feet at once.

"Ho there, this fine morning," he cried, beginning to run on the spot and every so often doing an arms-upward stretch. "Why so glum?" "Well," said the keelieworm, "I seem to be a bit out of condition. Have

80

you any suggestions for sprucing myself up a bit?" The jumping jeck did a quick handstand. "For a start, you'd need to get rid of some of that fat," he said. "How about a dozen or so press-ups first thing in the morning, and some deep breathing exercises? Then a quick gallop round the garden before breakfast – and that's another thing – breakfast. No stodgy rolls and marmalade: just a glass of lemon juice. I guarantee that will ease off a good few pounds in a week or so. And you'll have to do something about those legs and feet – exercise sandals. They're just the thing. You'll have ankles like a racehorse in a month." And the jumping jeck did a fast knees-bend-arms-akimbo bit, before sprinting lightly up the path.

The keelieworm felt quite exhausted merely watching him. "That would certainly be the end of me. If I could only find a nice quiet spot where I could lie down, I'm sure I'd feel better after a little sleep." She got up on her hind legs and peered hopefully about for a sheltered corner. At last she spied a narrow cranny under the ledge of a window and with a great deal of trouble the keelieworm made her way up over the wall until she reached the spot.

She settled herself comfortably and closed her eyes. A long rest would do her the world of good, and when she woke she'd start in earnest and really make the most of herself. Soon she fell into a deep sleep and she slept and she slept and she slept. And as she slept she dreamed.

She dreamed she was the loveliest creature in the whole wide garden. Light as air, floating and gliding over the summer blossoms. So she dreamed away the whole long winter, till at last, in the first warm spring sunshine, she woke.

And do you know – it hadn't been a dream at all. While she slept, she had changed into a beautiful butterfly, and she *was* the loveliest creature in the whole wide garden.

The Sly Goose

Once upon a time, long ago, in a peedie house over the
rim of the Heathery Hill, where the teebro runs forever,
there lived an old man. For company he had a great
spotted leather-back and Rhodie, the brown hen, who
had five fluffy chickens.

Each morning when the first beams of the sun
touched the spiders' webs among the heather and
turned them into gold, he'd get up and share his
breakfast with the great spotted leather-back; then
he'd sprinkle some grain and meal for Rhodie and her
chickens, and set off over the stony brae to the great
Heathery Hill, to cut peats.

One day, when he was digging and delving in the
peat bank, he came upon a rabbit hole, which was not
really unusual. But when he looked at it more closely, he
discovered, some way in, an old sly goose sitting on her
eggs.

Each day he had a look at the nest, till at last the
time came when the eggs had hatched out, all except
one. Soon the baby birds were strong enough to follow
their mother, and one morning, long before the old
man had got up, she led her brood down through the
heathery clump to the sea, and he never saw them again.

That day, after the old man had cut a great
mountain of peats, he lay down close to the nest and
rested a while. After a time he was sure he could hear
something squeaking close by, and he looked about this
way and that to discover what it could be. At last he

remembered the nest, and there was the remaining egg, with the baby bird just breaking through the shell.

When the time came for the old man to go home, he looked again at the baby sly goose, which was now safely out of the egg, and all dried and fluffy in the still warm nest. He knew that if he left it there it would die of cold when night came, so he slipped it into his pocket and carried it home.

The great spotted leather-back was waiting for him on the doorstep, where he had been sleeping all day in the sun, and he purred round the old man's ankles while he made the tea, and wondered what he'd do with the baby sly goose.

All at once he remembered that Rhodie and her chickens had still not been fed, so he hurried out to look for grain and meal for them; and when he was sprinkling it out in their dish, he had a most splendid idea. He took the baby sly goose from his pocket and popped it beneath Rhodie's warm feathers, where it snuggled down at once.

After a few days it was picking about with the chickens as if it had always been there, and old Rhodie never seemed to notice he was different from the rest of her babies, with his big flat feet and his broad beak, with which he shovelled up twice as much food as the others.

Soon the time came when the peedie sly goose was no longer content to stay with old Rhodie and her chickens, and it was not long before he started to wander off, and soon found the rest of the sly geese, puddling among the rocks and the pools, which was just as it should be.

The Silver Fishes

Long ago, when the world was young and troubles were few, when the sun shone forever and the river lay warm and green, there, along the quiet shore, lived a shoal of silver fishes.

All day long they darted and dived among the swaying water-weeds, skimming the gravel on the riverbed, and gliding through the dappled shadows.

"No other fish so fine as we," they sang as they played in the dark green caves beneath the willowy fronds. "None so fine," as they quivered and spun in the swirling water.

So they played and sang for many a day till the time grew short and the far sea called them, down through the swift river, over the foaming waterfalls, and into the quiet waters where the river met the sea.

The silver shoal turned eagerly into the salty sea, leaping and curving on their way to the Far North Land, far and away across the tilting ocean, glittering and gleaming through foaming surge.

"Whither away fine fishes?" called a shimmerous shark as he idled in the green surf. "Whither away?" he called again; but never a word they spoke as they darted into the shadowy distance, over the ocean meadows where the cope-pods trailed their shimmering scarves, over the crusted rocks and into the icy waters of the Far North Land.

There, under the creaking ice-fields, they lived while the season turned, feasting on shrimp and prawn in the crystal grottoes, and growing fat and sleek, till once again they heard the call from the riverbeds of home.

Eagerly, the silver fishes plunged once more into the wild waves, beyond the otter, rocking and drowsing among the kelp, and onward to where the white shark and the porpoise lay in wait.

Onward still across the wide sea, till they came again to the river of home, and upwards through the twinkling rushing water, through the pebbly shallows, back to the quiet green shore where they were born.

Transportation

"For the bate o' that," cried the Muckle Grullyan, throwing down *The Orcadian* in disgust and addressing no one in particular, chiefly because there was no one there to address, but more chiefly because he had gotten into the habit, as the Americans say, of talking to himself and that's a difficult habit to grow out of, like many another.

"For the bate o' that," he repeated, retrieving the scattered pages and re-reading the offending paragraph. Not only were "THEY" putting up air and sea fares, but, a much more heinous crime in his opinion, "THEY" were cancelling his own particular bus run into the town, an amenity of which he had been taking advantage more and more frequently with the passing years. Ah well, there would be nothing else for it but to get out the brogues and the staff and make the journey on foot, even though it was a distance of several miles. He was still musing over the calamity when he suddenly remembered an ancient bicycle that had been around the place after the war. Hopefully, it must still be in the shed, and with nothing much else to do, he went to dig it out.

Like most sheds, it was pretty well jam-packed with old mangles, leather work machines, and bits of broken car engine, so it was some time before he got a space cleared to move about in, and after being engulfed by several avalanches of half empty paint tins and lengths of felt, he began to suspect that some criminal had purloined the velocipede. There was simply no

sign of it. Almost at once, however, he recalled that, in
an attempt to preserve the tyres he had suspended the
machine from the roof, and sure enough, on peering
up into the gloom, there it hung in the aisons, fearfully
enveloped in cobwebs and dust, but seemingly intact.

Getting it down was no easy task, but finally after
a great deal of expended energy, it was lowered to the
ground and he wheeled it triumphantly outside. Flakes
of rust fell like red dandruff from the machine, but after
a sharp kick or two, most of it was loosened. Amazingly,
the bicycle was in working order. A slight stiffness of the
brakes perhaps, but that was little odds. Even the leather
bag on the back of the saddle still held a few spanners
and a yellow Dunlop tin with some chalk and a length of
valve tubing. Even more amazing, a large carbide lamp
was still firmly clamped to the handlebars.

It was empty of course, and the Muckle Grullyan
almost smiled as he remembered terrifying the peedie
buckies by setting fire to a mound of carbide on a
long ago Guy Fawkes night. He leaned the bicycle up
against the wall and set about it with a large can of oil
and a rag, and in very little time it began to look almost
roadworthy. A flock of tourists, scantily dressed in shorts
and sunglasses, cycled bravely across his inner vision.
He just might invest in a pair of sunglasses when he
hit town. The cost, set aside the astronomical bus fares
he had been paying, would be minimal, and there was
really quite a glare off the roads these days.

"Well, that seems to be it," he said at last,
throwing down the oil can and the rag. A quick burst
round the house, just to get his hand in, so to speak,

and then he'd be off to the town. He pointed the bicycle hopefully in the direction of the road and swinging his leg carefully over the saddle, he wobbled slowly down the track towards the main road.

"My chove," he thought, standing on the pedals as he laboured up the steepening hill behind the house, "this is a sight more tiring than sitting in a bus, but then, think of the good it must be doing. The exercise must be almost as beneficial as yoga." Still, he was quite glad when he turned out on to the main road and began to run smoothly down the hill into town, the soldiers on the side of the road rattling their heads merrily against the spokes as he flew past.

By this time, he had got up quite a turn of speed, with the wind whistling past his ears and bringing the water to his eyes, so that it was some moments before he realised he was being flagged down by a passing car. The rusted brakes proved to be immovable, so he was forced to drag his foot along the road, sending up showers of flinty sparks, but alas, long before he could bring the speeding machine to a decent stop, his foot hit a large tussock of grass, throwing him and his bicycle in a brullyo almost under the wheels of the car.

Slowly he began to extricate himself from the wreckage, making as he did so the somewhat cheering discovery that at least the carbide lamp was whole. Only then did he become aware of the policeman by his side, flexing his writing arm, and making menacing gestures with his notebook. Glancing over the man's shoulder as he was assisted on his way, he caught a glimpse of the first few notes in the book, beginning with "Excess speed," "Faulty brakes," "Unroadworthy machine," and going on almost to the bottom of the page. He wondered idly if he would be allowed to read *The Orcadian* in prison.

The Lickull Piggie

Old Mother Pig had produced twelve simply beautiful little piglets, all pink and fat and covered in silky down, with round cheeky noses and long silvery eyelashes. They behaved perfectly, and laid themselves in a neat row to drink their milk without the least bit of bother. No pushing or shoving or anything like that. However, there had to be some little fault, and of course there was… The Lickull Piggie.

He was wrinkled and skinny, and his legs were wobbly, but worst of all, he was troublesome. His mother knew at once that he was going to be a problem so she was especially firm with him, but to little avail. He trod on his brothers and sisters, he squealed, he pushed, he shoved and, horror of horrors, he actually bit one of them, right on the end of his snout, leaving his sharp little teeth marks for all to see. Then he climbed up over their backs where they all lay drinking their milk, digging his small hard trotters into them. Without a care, he then stamped straight up over his mother and right on to the sloping roof of the pig sty. Mother Pig was furious, but of course she was not able to get at him at that precise moment, since the rest of the little piggies were busy drinking their milk, but she glared at him, and do you know, that awful Lickull Piggie paid not the slightest heed, but continued to walk further up the roof till he was able to see right over the top, and away across the farmyard. Mother Pig was in such a rage. "Come down from there at once!" she shouted, "you will fall

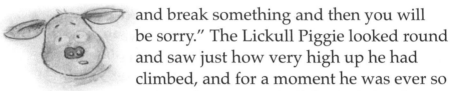and break something and then you will be sorry." The Lickull Piggie looked round and saw just how very high up he had climbed, and for a moment he was ever so slightly worried. Mother Pig and all the little brothers and sisters were gazing up at him in great alarm. Then, to everyone's amazement, he spread out his front trotters, and then his back trotters and finally his ears, and flew calmly back to the ground. Well really, whoever heard of such a thing? A flying piglet!

Mother Pig was so angry. "You stupid little piglet," she bellowed at him, "don't you realise you are not supposed to do that? You are not a bird, or a butterfly, or anything of that sort. You are a piglet, and piglets *Do Not Fly*, so I want no more nonsense of that kind, if you please," and she hustled him back into the sty with all the other little piglets where they burrowed down into the straw and fell asleep. Except, of course, the Lickull Piggie. He lay awake for simply ages, tossing and turning and being perfectly bothersome. Soon it became dark, and then, oddly enough, a silvery sort of light began to shine in through a crack in the door, and The Lickull Piggie, being extremely curious as well as everything else, got up to investigate, treading over his brothers and sisters as he did so. He put his eye to the crack in the door and there, high in the sky, shone the moon. "How perfectly splendid," thought The Lickull Piggie, "as soon as I can get out of here I am going to fly right up there, no matter what Mother Pig says, I am going to do it. In the meantime I had better get some rest." He trotted over to where his brothers and sisters were snoring and snuffling in the straw and fell asleep.

Next morning he woke as soon as it was daylight. Someone had opened the door of the pigsty and emptied a great bucket full of swill into the trough for Mother Pig. She lumbered up out of the straw to get her breakfast. The Lickull Piggie peered over the top of the trough to see what she was eating. It looked utterly disgusting. Watery milk, bits of cabbage and bits of eggshells floating around in it and all sorts of stuff like leftover potato and stale bread. Not a pretty sight, but Mother Pig didn't seem to mind and made the most hideous and vulgar noise as she guzzled around in the trough. All this time The Lickull Piggie was gazing around at the sky and becoming more and more alarmed. There was not a sign of the lovely moon he had seen the night before. "The moon," he cried, "the lovely moon, it's gone." And he made such a weeping and wailing the Mother Pig interrupted her breakfast to give him a sharp clip on the ear. "Be quiet," she bellowed, "you stupid boy. The moon doesn't come out in the daylight – well, not so you would notice anyway, so what is all the fuss about?" She glared fiercely at The Lickull Piggie with great lumps of curdled milk and bits of cabbage dripping off her chin, then heedlessly went on eating her breakfast.

The old milk cow hung her head over the wall. "Let me explain," she said in a gentle voice to The Lickull Piggie, and proceeded to clarify for him some of the mysteries of the universe. "I would like to go up there," squeaked The Lickull Piggie, his eyes shining. "Well, you never know" said the old milk cow, "perhaps when you have grown a bit." She smiled. "What a pleasant little fellow he is," she said to Mother Pig, who was scratching herself on the wall of the pigsty. "I think he may go far, although such an adventurous spirit might be rather a handicap." She smiled once more and then trundled away across the yard, leaving Mother Pig settling down again to the task of feeding her brood. The Lickull Piggie could hardly wait for night to come, and when they arrived in the evening to close the door of the pigsty, he hid himself by the side of the trough and no one noticed he wasn't safely tucked away with the rest of the piggies.

As soon as it was dark, The Lickull Piggie crept from his hiding place, then he climbed over the trough, on to the wall, and up the sloping roof. The moon was just rising, a great yellow ball in the sky. The Lickull Piggie was so excited, but rather scared as well, because he had no idea exactly how to set about this great adventure. Presently, he heard a scuffling and a squeaking in the grass by the wall, and two long lean rats came scampering out of the shadows. "Hi there Lickull Piggie" they squeaked, "what's afoot, shouldn't you be in bed?" "Well no," said the Lickull Piggie, "I am just about to fly to the moon, but I am not quite certain of the way." He looked down at the rats and they stared back up at him and then fell about on the ground, laughing and hitting each other's shoulders. "Flying is it?" and they laughed even more loudly. "Take our advice and ask the old Hooty Owl down in the plantation. He will be able to set you off in the right direction." "Thank you," cried The Lickull Piggie, "I will do just that," and to the astonishment of the rats, he spread out his front trotters and then his back trotters and finally his ears, and sailed away over the high stone wall of the farmyard towards the plantation.

While this was going on, the moon climbed higher in the sky and lit up the whole countryside with her silvery light, and as he flew along The Lickull Piggie could see all sorts of creatures out and about, much more so than in the daylight. Flocks of bats flitted by, and myriads of night moths drifted over the tall grasses. Families of field mice swung about among the corn stalks in the grain fields, and in the thick undergrowth he could hear the hedgehogs bumbling around choosing the largest of the big black slugs and snails that had come out to sip the dew. Many of these creatures called out to The Lickull Piggie as he passed overhead, but he paid no heed as he flew towards the plantation, never stopping for a second. He had no idea where to look for Hooty Owl, and the trees of the plantation loomed large and dark before him. Great leafy branches reached out to catch him as he passed, and long swathes of ivy and honeysuckle became entangled in his ears and round his little trotters. Just when he had decided to fly higher up and over the trees there was a soft rush of wings overhead, and the Hooty Owl dropped onto a tree branch just in front of him. It was quite a large branch, and The Lickull Piggie was able to squeeze himself alongside the Hooty Owl. Hooty Owl had caught a vole and he hung this on a nearby branch and turned his head to speak to The Lickull Piggie, his huge round golden eyes glowing in the light of the moon.

The Lickull Piggie felt quite alarmed. Hooty Owl looked so very fierce, and kept twisting his head round and round, so that at any moment The Lickull Piggie expected to see it fall onto the ground and roll away out of sight under the trees. No such thing occurred, and The Lickull Piggie began to realize it must be a trick of the light, or some such thing, that made the owl's head appear to twist right round. He gave up worrying about it, and listened carefully to what Hooty Owl had to say.

The way to the moon was quite clear. You only had to look up and follow the shining way. The problem was, the moon would keep getting bigger and smaller, and sometimes even disappearing altogether so no one ever knew from one night till the next exactly what size it would be, or even exactly where it would be. Very confusing. "Why don't you go to the sun instead?" asked Hooty Owl. "That's always there, and though it does move around a bit, it is far more predictable than the moon, and of course you must also take into account the fact that the earth is moving as well. "Excuse me," The Lickull Piggie interrupted. "Let's not get too technical about all this. I only want to take a simple, straightforward trip, I mean to say, there it is, up there, plain to be seen. No problem surely?" "Well I suppose you could be right," agreed Hooty Owl. "They tell me that a bit of cloud is all that might trouble you, and apparently the further away you get from the earth, the less cloud there is. None at all in some cases I believe, but I can't be certain of that, because I have never really been further than the plantation. Never felt the need, if you understand."

Hooty Owl looked at The Lickull Piggie. His eyes seemed larger than ever, so that The Lickull Piggie began to wonder if he was doing the right thing after all, but when he looked up through the branches, there was the moon, shining as silvery bright as ever, and he knew for certain that was where he wanted to go, so he thanked the Hooty Owl for his advice, and off he went once more, skimming over the trees, till he came to the far boundary of the plantation. Away into the distance the little hills and valleys stretched to the horizon, and when he screwed up his eyes and looked very hard he thought he could see far and far away, a line of shining silver. It must surely be the path to the moon.

All through the night The Lickull Piggie flew on. Over the fields and meadows, where the long grasses hung heavy with the falling dew. Over the streams and rivers that shone and glittered in the moonlight. Over the quaking marsh where the green frogs sang in the night. On and on he flew. He was so tired, his ears and trotters ached with cold because a little frost had stung the glittering countryside and it seemed that he was flying through the land of the fairies, with the moon clear and bright ahead. He had just begun to think that he might have to turn back he was so tired, when he saw that he had come to the brink of a great shining lake, and gleaming across the water lay the moon path. The moon itself had dipped low, almost to the surface of the lake. If only he could keep going for just a little longer, he knew, he just knew, he could reach the great shining moon.

Lower and lower he drifted, his little ears and trotters almost too tired to go any further. Then he was in the water, falling down through the green deeps, and the moon, a great shining ring was all around him. He had made it. He had reached the moon at last. But how was he to escape from the cold waters of the lake? The waterweed and grasses clung round him, pulling him down and down into the dark deeps. Shining bubbles flew round him, and just when he was drifting down for the last time, Bruck the otter, sleek and brown and powerful, swept him up in a shower of bubbles and carried him on to the bank, safe and sound.

The moon had long gone and in the east the clouds were edged with gold. The Lickull Piggie knew he would never be able to fly all the way back home again. He lay on the soft grass by the lake shore, thinking of all his adventures and began to wish he was safely back home with his brothers and sisters and, worse than that, he was beginning to feel more than a bit hungry, and not a scrap of food to be had.

After a time The Lickull Piggie became aware of a lip-lapping in the water. He sat up and looked around. Sailing by, like a great ship, was a snowy white swan. Suddenly, with a powerful sweep of his black feet he swung himself round towards the bank and climbed slowly up out of the water and looked down at The Lickull Piggie. "You are a piggie!" said the swan in a very surprised voice, "I haven't seen a piggie in ages. How come you are here at this time in the morning?" "Actually," said The Lickull Piggie, "I flew, but it was such a long journey I don't think I'd care to do it again. I wanted to fly to the moon you see." "And did you?" asked the swan. "I certainly did," grinned The Lickull Piggie, "and I caught it just here in the lake." "That's the way of it indeed," said the white swan, "but you know, not a lot of people understand that."

For a while they both sat silently by the shore of the lake. "Would you care for a lift back home?" asked the white swan presently, and he lifted up his feathers so that they made a very comfortable nest. "I often carry my babies this way," he said, "but only on the lake." He waddled slowly back into the water and with great long strides of his black feet he took off and they flew swiftly away into the sunrise.

Oddly enough, when The Lickull Piggie arrived back home, not a one had missed him. He climbed quickly down off the roof and into the sty. Mother Pig was gobbling her breakfast as greedily as usual. All the other little piggies were still fast asleep, and only the old milk cow seemed in the least bit interested to see him back home, but then, she knew all about the moon and how to get there.

Some weeks later, on a beautiful sunny day, the farmer and his man came to open the field gate so that Mother Pig could run free for a time in the buttercup meadow. As usual The Lickull Piggie, curious as ever, stopped to listen to what the farmer and his man were talking about. "Hurry up there" cried the Mother Pig, "no dawdling behind or you will get lost in the long grass as sure as eggs is eggs...come on...hurry along." The Lickull Piggie for once did as he was told, and trotted quickly along to catch up with his brothers and sisters. "I say," he panted as he ran up beside his mother, "what's pork?" Mother Pig stopped so abruptly that all the little piggies fell over each other. "Murssy Me!" she gasped, "I can't believe I heard that! That's a very naughty word and I don't want to hear you using it again...Ever!" She glared ferociously at The Lickull Piggie and gave him a sharp push with her snout, before setting off once more through the grass.

"Well, is bacon a naughty word as well? Because I heard the farmer saying..." He got no further, old Mother Pig gave him such a clip on the ear. "How dare you listen to other people's conversations, it's dreadfully rude...and yes...that also is a very bad word, even worser in fact." Mother Pig was in such a rage, flapping her cheeks and breathing very heavily. The Lickull Piggie hung his head and slunk away among the tall dochans by the edge of the field, and sulked for a time. He was always getting himself into trouble, through no fault of his own that he could see. After a while he began to rootle about among the tangled weeds and grasses, brooding upon the consequences of having an enquiring mind.

Presently he came upon a sagging wooden fence, and, pushing himself through a gap in the planks, he found he was in a neat little garden. The beds were full

100

of all kinds of beautiful flowers and shrubs of every colour you could imagine, and here and there tall trees threw long cool shadows across the paths. The grass was neatly cut and as The Lickull Piggie wandered down a shady path he discovered a marvellous vegetable garden, with long rows of succulent vegetables growing, lush and green. Suddenly he realised he had become quite hungry. The problem was – what to eat first? He crunched up a tasty little cabbage, and then had a quick nibble of one of the most delicious cauliflowers he had ever tasted. He was just about to have even more when he spied, just out of reach, a cluster of fat green peapods. He reached up on his tippy toes to capture a long branch that was simply weighed down with luscious pods, when to his great surprise one of the peas opened its eyes and yawned! The Lickull Piggie stepped back in amazement. It wasn't a pea at all. Curled up in the peapod was a fairy baby. Thank goodness he had noticed in time or the little thing could have been swallowed without a trace.

He began to look about more carefully, and as he peered into all the flowers and plants, he discovered that almost every one sheltered a tiny fairy creature. They were all mostly fast asleep for they were very young, but he soon became aware that the place was simply alive with fairies. They were peering at him from behind every clump of flowers, hanging from branches, and even as he looked, a very bold one came striding up the path towards him. He was ringing a tiny bell that he carried in his hand and The Lickull Piggie knew at once that he must be a very important little person, and so it turned out.

"Ho there, Lickull Piggie" cried the very important little person, in a very small voice. "We've been keeping a very close eye on you, rooting about in our garden. How come you are not with the rest of the piggies in the buttercup meadow?" "Well," said The Lickull Piggie sadly, "it was all because I said a naughty word, and really I was only asking what it meant, not actually using it, if you see what I mean, and Mother Pig was so angry she sent me off in disgrace. She's always doing that. It's because I have an enquiring mind you see." "So I've noticed," replied the very important little person. "We don't often have individuals breaking in and eating us out of house and home." "Well, I truly am sorry," said The Lickull Piggie, "how was I to know I wasn't supposed to eat the stuff? No one seems to want to tell me anything."

As he said this, he began to feel quite depressed and, to his horror, great tears came into his eyes and rolled down his cheeks. "Now now," said the important little person, "there's no need to get in a state, a few mouthfuls of cabbage aren't going to bankrupt us. By the way," he continued, "how did you manage to find your way into the garden? It's a secret garden you know, and there is no way in." "Well now," said The Lickull Piggie, "it was down by that patch of dochans on the way to the plantation. There is a gap in the planks and I just sort of fell through." "Dear oh dear," cried the important little person. "We must get that repaired at once. We can't have every Tom, Dick or Harry dropping in unannounced. Perhaps you could do that for us in your spare time?" "Well I have plenty of that," said The Lickull Piggie. "I used to fly quite a lot you know, but I have had to give it up, I seem to have got too heavy for it as I have grown older, and I am lucky if I can manage even a little gliding nowadays." "What a pity," said the very important little person. "I can't think how we would manage if we couldn't fly. Have you got any plans for the future? What are you going to do when you grow up for instance?" "Yes - well that is a problem," said The Lickull Piggie. "There is not a lot of scope for a piggie nowadays. Everything is computerized." "Yes indeed," agreed the very important little person, "we have the same sort of problem. There is simply no call for having rags changed into ball gowns and very few princesses needing to be rescued. In fact I haven't even seen a princess in ages. Very scarce they are nowadays, and even if you do come across one, they are hardly ever in distress."

As they were talking, The Lickull Piggie became aware of a most delicious aroma. It seemed to be coming from beneath the oak tree under which they were sitting and he looked all round but there was nothing to be seen, except the neatly cut grass around the base of the tree. "Excuse me," he interrupted the very important little person, who had continued talking of this and that. "What is that delicious smell? It seems to be all around just here." "Well now" said the very important little person, "could it be that you are smelling the truffles? Not a lot of people can do that, you know. It is a bit like water divining, an art given to a chosen few. If you can find where the truffles are hidden you would be invaluable to anyone in the truffle trade. Have a little sniff around and see what you can find." As you can imagine, The Lickull Piggie needed no second bidding and in next to no time he had traced the truffles and had dug up several fat clumps. "Well there you are then," cried the very important little person. "As soon as the farmer hears about this he'll have you down in the plantation digging the truffles like crazy. That's where they mostly are you know, down in the plantation, beneath the oak trees. We only have a few here in the garden for our own personal use you understand."

For a while, they went on talking, until the shadows grew long across the garden, but before The Lickull Piggie returned home they repaired the gap in the wooden fence, so that no one else could stumble into the secret garden.

As you can imagine The Lickull Piggie lost no time in letting the farmer know that he was no ordinary piglet, but a truffle pig, and in a very short time he was given a red harness with a bell and a long leather lead so that he could take the farmer truffle hunting in the plantation. Sometimes as they wandered beneath the trees The Lickull Piggie would see the faintest glimmer in the shadows, and hear the ring of a tiny bell and catch a glimpse of the very important little person flitting among the branches.

And so the troublesome Lickull Piggie was now a very clever Lickull Piggie, and Mother Pig was very, very proud of him.

Day Trip

Tony was going to the County Show, and it was still not daylight when his mother woke him up to get washed and dressed. He was quite puzzled at first to be awakened so early, until he remembered where he was going, and then he flew out of bed in a trice.

He was ready before his mother and sisters, and waited outside the door in a fever of impatience. They were travelling by sea, and the big cargo ship lay at the pier just below the house. It would be quite a long journey, because they had to call at four other islands on the way to collect passengers from each, so they had to start very early, at six o'clock.

The gangway ran steeply up to the deck, so Tony had to hold firmly to the rail as they all climbed aboard. They chose a seat by the window, inside the cabin, because there was a sharp cold wind blowing, and they watched the strong ropes being cast off and the looped ends splashing heavily into the water as the ship swung away from the pier. Soon they were out of the harbour and heaving through choppy waves on the open sea.

A crowd of people were waiting at their first port of call, and they soon came on board, filling the upper cabin with baskets and prams and the like, and when they were all seated the big ship continued on her way.

After a time, they came close in by the land and Tony saw two little boats waiting in the shallows. Could it be smugglers? The boats came puttering out, throwing clouds of spray on either side. As they drew near, Tony could see the names on their sides – the *Cutty Sark* and the *Osprey*. Surely they must be smugglers! But no, they had only ordinary passengers on board, who climbed hurriedly in through the cargo doors on the ship's side, leaving the little boats to scurry back to the shore, while the big ship sailed swiftly on, passing close by the steep red cliffs where the seabirds clustered like snow on the ledges, and the waves foamed over the rocks.

Soon, the sea grew very rough and great waves soared up along the ship's sides, and Tony began to feel sick, so they went outside into the fresh air and he leaned his head on the rail and felt better.

Before long, they reached the last two islands. All the passengers embarked and they were on the last stage of the journey. They passed a deserted island, with wild sheep grazing down to the water's edge, and over the hill the towers of a castle came up against the sky. Tony looked and looked for soldiers on horseback, or a battle, or a knight of old, but there was none.

By this time, they had reached the end of their journey and everyone streamed off the ship, and went about their business. Tony was hungry, so they all had something to eat, and then went shopping, and climbed the stone stairs to see the handicrafts. Tony was not really interested in the fine sewing and quilted cushions, so he leaned over the railings to watch the pipers getting ready. They blew on their pipes till the arched walls rang with the din, and their bright buckled tartans gleamed as they swung through the high door.

The streets outside were thronged with eager crowds, and they joined the hurrying stream moving towards the show park. By the gates of the park was a man with a monkey. When Tony held the tiny creature, it curled its little gnarled hand in his and looked wistfully over his shoulder at the passing crowd. Tony felt sure it must be cold, although it wore a woollen jersey against the chill wind.

Inside the gate were the two biggest dogs in the whole wide world. They were sleek and brown and shivered with excitement as they strained at their leads. Tony felt it best not to pet them in case they were inclined to have his arm off in one bite, so he wandered off with the others to see the ponies, tethered in their pens by the wall. One little white one, with black streaky spots, sprang about like a fury, kicking at the fence and leaping over the gate, so that his mistress had to cling to his lead rope and shout to everyone to stand back. Tony liked it better than the fat black ponies standing stolidly near by.

In the ring, all the prize-winning animals lumbered heavily around with ribbons fluttering. A great red bull with long horns, and white curls round his ears, rolled his eyes ferociously, so they quickly stepped back and hastened down the field to see the sheep in their narrow pens. Some were ordinary old grey things, but a few had their fleeces dyed a brilliant yellow, and two fat beauties were coloured a deep brown. When Tony pressed his hand lightly on their backs, their wool felt like softest velvet. Presently the big trucks backed into the pens and the sheep were loaded in and driven slowly away through the crowds.

For a time, they stayed to watch the ponies

trotting and jumping, but the wind that blew across the grass was cold and bitter, so they left the noisy park behind and went down through the streets for tea.

Soon it was time to go. They bought sticky sweets and a shaggy coconut, and some books to read on the way. The big ship waited at the pier. Tony's legs were hardly able to carry him up the gangway, and when they found a seat in the cabin, he laid his head on his mother's knee and fell fast asleep, and he slept until home was just in sight over the darkening sea.

The Peedie Herdie Boy

Once upon a time in the olden days when the fields
had no fine fences and the roads were rutted and stony,
there was a peedie herdie boy. He lived all alone with
his mother, and they were very poor, because his father
had died when he was only a baby, so as soon as he was
old enough his mother sent him out to work at a nearby
farm as a herdie boy.

Each morning, on his bare brown feet, he would
set off up the hillside with the cattle. He carried a stout
stick, and over his shoulder hung an old canvas bag,
which held a flask of water to drink, and a few oatcakes
with a lump of cheese to eat. Sometimes, if the farmer's
wife was in a generous mood, she'd give him milk
instead of water, and on those days he would think he
was a very lucky peedie boy as he drank the creamy
milk and ate his oatcakes and cheese on the windy
hillside.

But sometimes he would think he was not so
lucky, when the wind blew bitterly from the east,
whistling through the thistles and the thin grass, and
then he would huddle into his ragged cloak and fold his
bare feet together to keep warm.

When he came home in the evening, the peedie
boy would be tired and weary, and his bare feet would
be cut and scratched with trampling over the rough
hillside after the cattle. His mother would have his
supper ready for him, and she would have a big round
smooth stone from the seashore warming in the hot

ashes of the peat fire to put in his bed of heather and soft moss, to keep him warm through the night.

One evening, when he returned tired and cold with the cattle from the hillside, he saw that his master had a visitor, a rich merchant from the town. As the peedie boy went by, he looked at the merchant's splendid leather boots. Some day, he thought to himself, he might have boots like that and be able to tramp the stony roads without a care.

The merchant took his leave of the farmer, climbed into his carriage and drove away. At that moment, the peedie herdie boy saw that the merchant had dropped his big leather purse, so he picked it up and ran, shouting as loudly as he could, after the carriage.

The merchant heard him, and reined in his horses; but just as the peedie herdie boy reached him, he caught his foot on a sharp stone, and down he fell. He scrambled up at once, dashing away the tears of pain as he held up the purse. But the merchant had seen that the peedie boy's foot was cut, and felt very sorry for him, so he searched in his purse for a penny as a reward.

When the peedie herdie boy reached home that night and gave his mother the penny, was he not the proudest peedie fellow? In those days a penny could buy many things.

But the merchant could not forget the peedie herdie boy. He kept remembering the tears in the peedie boy's eyes and the blood from his cut foot on the dusty road. At last he persuaded himself that he really needed the boy to help tend his horses and his gardens, so he made up his mind to ask the farmer if the boy could come and work for him instead.

The farmer agreed to let him go, and the peedie herdie boy started work with his new master. Never again did he feel the chill of the cold biting wind, and never again were his bare feet cut and scratched on the rough roads, for his new master provided him with thick warm clothes and a pair of stout leather boots, so he could tramp the stony road without a care.

The Great North Wind

Once upon a time there stood a high headland with huge craggy cliffs, and the wide grey sea stretching away in front to the rim of the world. It was a bleak and lonely place with only the sound of the sea and the call of the seabirds to break the silence, but it was the favourite playground of The Great North Wind, who loved to come swooping down from the ice fields of the Far North Land where the Merry Dancers swing and flicker over the frozen wastelands, roaring and whining as he blew among the desolate crags and across the bleak moor.

Then one day, as he swept in from the sea in a cloud of rain and salt spray, he discovered that someone had built a peedie house on the very rim of the headland. The Great North Wind was furious, and roared round the house in a great rage, shaking the doors and windows and howling in the chimney, trying to find a crack or a cranny where he could squeeze in and blow down the peedie grey house, for he wanted no one to share his favourite playground.

But not a crack or a cranny could he find, and the windows were all tightly fastened against him. When he looked into the peedie grey house, he saw that an old woman lived there, and although she seemed harmless enough, he still could not bear to see anyone living there, so he made up his mind to be rid of her as soon as ever he could.

Every day he blew and raged round the peedie house trying to prise up the shingles with his long fingers, or creep in under the door, but the peedie house was so firmly built that he tried in vain.

By and by, he grew tired of raging, and blew away out over the sea, tossing the clouds and vanishing away to the Far North Land to plan and think. At last he decided that storming and raging were doing no good at all, so he crept back in over the sea with only a shiver on the water to mark his path, hoping to catch the old woman unawares and creep in by an open window; but still they were all tightly closed, and although he waited and watched for many days, never once did she leave them open.

Then one day, the old woman went out to gather sticks for her fire, leaving her little granddaughter alone to look after the house. When The Great North Wind saw this, he rushed in over the sea, roaring and raging, thinking to frighten the little girl into opening a window, but the louder he blew, the tighter she closed it, so at last he gave up, and grumbled and growled away back out over the sea once more. Then he began to creep slowly back in, riffling the water with the lightest of breezes, sighing over the crags with a whisper, slipping round the peedie grey house till he came to a window.

The little girl looked out, but she didn't see The Great North Wind. She saw only the sun glinting on the water, and the seabirds gliding and swooping in the still air, so she opened wide the window, and leaned out. At once, The Great North Wind sprang up and swept into the peedie grey house, blowing aside the frilly white curtains, and filling the room with his icy breath. He was just about to sweep the peedie grey house into the sea with a great gust of wind when his eye was caught by the dancing flames of the fire. He looked around him and saw what a cosy place it was, with pretty dishes on the dresser, and a furry black cat curled up on the chair by the fire. He began to think it would be a shame to destroy such a pleasant place after all, and surely the old woman must love the lonely place as much as he, to build her home there, so he decided to leave the peedie house just as it was, and slipped quietly out through the window once more, drifting down over the craggy rocks and away out over the sea to the Far North Land.

The March of the Snowmen

Once upon a time, one night in the long dark winter, it became increasingly cold so that everybody had to get up and scrabble about in the ottoman at the foot of their beds to get another blanket, and when daylight came and the curtains were drawn back, the children saw that there had been a fall of snow.

It had covered the garden, piled in fleecy drifts up along the walls and encrusted the dykes and fences. The old bhour trees along the top lawn looked like a silvery fairy forest with every branch glittering white.

Then the children noticed that under the drooping laburnum tree there stood a big fat snowman. He seemed to be listening for something, and as they watched, he lifted his hand to shade his eyes, looking and looking this way and that, into the far white morning.

The children flew downstairs and gobbled their breakfast. They bundled themselves up in thick scarves and gloves and balaclavas and wellingtons and duffel coats and crunched out into the shining morning, moagsing up the path to where the snowman watched and waited under the old laburnum tree.

He was a splendid fellow, fat and round, but he was rather worried because he had dropped off to sleep during the night and was afraid that he might have missed the rest of the snowmen who had begun their march back to the Far North Land where they spent the summer. They were due to pass this way at any time, and it would be a dreadful calamity to be left behind.

To undertake the journey alone was impossible because the way was long and hard and they needed the guidance of their stalwart leaders to encourage and cheer them on their way, with the merry music of their flutes and the steady beat of the drum.

All day the children played by the fat snowman. They built snow houses and dug paths and rolled snowballs and slid on the strip of ice down the side of the path, and all day the snowman watched and waited for his companions, looking and listening through the long cold hours.

At length it was teatime, and the children left their play and went in to tea. As they sat round the table in the window they could see the snowman still waiting under the old laburnum tree. Soon it began to grow dark, with great black clouds hurrying overhead, and a wild wind sprang up, blowing the snow till the garden was full of icy smoke. The snowman looked very sad and lonely so the children persuaded him to wait in the shelter of the porch, where he would be able to watch, safely out of the wind. Round his neck they wrapped one of Daddy's old scarves and to keep him from being lonely through the night, they left Pandi and The David Doll sitting by him on the windowsill in the porch.

All night long the snowman watched and waited, and all night long the wind blew, and it began to rain. The poor snowman was certain that he had indeed missed the rest of the company, and great tears began to slide down his icy cheeks.

Then at last the wind dropped and the stars came

out and, faint and far away in the distance, the snowman heard the beat of a drum and the high thin notes of a flute, and over the rim of the hill and down across the snowy meadow came the snowmen, row upon row, marching, marching on into the starry morning, their feet stamping through the snow and slush.

"Only just in time," thought the snowman, for already the snow was melting fast and soon it would have been too late. He took his place in the snowy ranks, and forward they marched under the glittering stars, forward to the Far North Land, the sound of the drum and the flute fading into the white yonder.

And in the morning, only Daddy's old scarf was left, with Pandi and The David Doll still watching and waiting by the window.

Winter

Once upon a time there was a storm, blowing up from the south-east and bringing the first breath of winter to the green islands, still bright with the flowers of a vanished summer.

Salt sea spray stung in the wind that roared in from the sea, scattering the withered leaves and bending the russet grasses by the roadsides till their proud tassels lay curved and broken.

Towards evening, their lost lonely cries floating down the wind, the wild geese came in on the gale, dropping like grey shadows to the shelter of the loch, where teal and widgeon had found refuge earlier in the day, and where the wild swans swung at anchor among the reeds.

A creamy breasted redstart, her scarlet tail feathers sadly ruffled, appeared in the garden and sought shelter in the tossing branches of the fuchsias. A flurry of gold-tipped brown leaves blew down the path and swirled up among the lower branches, changing like a miracle into a flock of tiny gold crests, clinging precariously among the twigs.

Darkness came early, the leaden sky vanishing in the murk, and as the night passed the wind increased in force, drowning the tinkling cries of the gold crests in its mighty roar.

At last the yellow light of morning crept up in the sky. Twigs and torn leaves flew in the gale, and the tiny gold crests were swept helplessly in its path. A furious gust of wind tossed them high along the wall, and they were carried over into the shelter of the corn yard where the wide doors of the hay shed stood partly open. The little flock flew in, dropping wearily onto the high beams of the shed and clustering over the sweet smelling hay. They filled the shed with their tinkling fairy voices as they preened their ruffled feathers and filled their starving bodies with fat hay seeds. The farmyard cats blinked their yellow eyes from their warm nest in the corner, but seemed to know that while the storm raged outside, peace must reign within, and they left the little feathered creatures to rest.

For many days the storm raged and no wild thing stirred. Waterfowl clustered among the singing reeds, their ghostly voices swept away on the gale. Little furry creatures slept the storm away in nest and burrow. All nature watched and waited till at last the howl died in the wind and faded slowly away. The lowering sky began to lift and the clouds flew higher into the west. With the dawning of a new day the little islands lay once more under a blue sky.

But it was not the warm blue sky of summer, it was the cold blue sky of winter. The buttercup fields lay stripped and black. No leaves hung in lacy green on the branches. The horned nasturtiums, which only a few short days ago had hung over the rough stone walls in a curtain of flame and yellow, now lay in blackened swathes along the garden wall.

Even the song of the sea had changed its tune from the warm chuckle of quiet water over silver sand and pebbles to the deep wild roar of foaming breakers

surging up under the cliffs.
  So soon had winter come.

To Celebrate The Birthday

Once upon a time, after a spell of bitterly cold weather, the Groolie Belkie decided that he would build himself a proper house, with doors and windows, and even a chimney. He had grown tired of living in his cold dark cave under the cliff, where it was cold and draughty, and when he lit a fire for warmth, it smoked and smouldered and filled the place with fumes and ashes. Now that he was getting older he felt the cold dreadfully in his creaking bones; so, all in all, he decided that he needed a new house.

Accordingly, all through the fine days of summer he carried the pink sea-washed stones up over the sloping shore to the banks above, and all through the fine days of summer he chipped and hammered and built and plastered till at length he had completed a sturdy dwelling. As soon as that was finished, he set about collecting a good supply of driftwood for his fire, and by the time winter had come he had a great pile of logs and bits of plank and tree branches and the like, all piled up to dry by the wall.

Each evening when he came home from tending his creels and lines he'd sit himself down by his wide fireplace and mend his nets and gear in the yellow light from the blazing driftwood, and think to himself what a fine house he had made, with not a draught, nor smoke, nor bit of damp in the walls.

By and by however, he began to miss the sound of the sea, like it used to be, bubbling and muttering in the doorway of his old dark cave, and he missed hearing the buckies and the grey limpets rattling and moving in the shallow pools by the wall; and most of all he missed the Peedie Sandlo poking and prying and hunting for titbits in the rocks and chingle near by. High above the shore in his grand new house he began to feel very lonely.

One day when he had made the rounds of his creels and nets, he found that there was more than the usual number broken and damaged, so he had to work far into the night mending and repairing. At last they were all finished and set in a neat row ready for the morning, and the Groolie Belkie threw a big log on the fire to be warm and cheery while he ate his supper.

As he sat there, he became aware of a scrabbling and thumping on the roof, and just when he was thinking that there must be rats nesting in the aisons, there was a great shower of soot and trevallie down through the wide chimney, and in a storm of smoke and sparks fell a fat old man wearing a long red cloak and clutching a half empty sack. The Groolie Belkie was astonished, to say the least, and he stared in amazement at the peedie man, who was stamping furiously on the edges of his cloak, which was smouldering dangerously.

"Heavens to Betsy!" cried the old man, dashing soot out of his beard and wiping his eyes. "What are you doing with such an aiser of a fire on at this time of night? I could have done myself a right mischief."

By this time the Groolie Belkie was beginning to think that the old fellow must be out of his mind, coming down the chimney when there was a perfectly

good door handy; so he said as much.

"But it's the custom, man," cried his visitor. "Personally I'd be only too glad to come in by the door. All this chimney climbing is becoming too much for me. I'm not so young any more."

"Do you mean to tell me that you are in the habit of doing this sort of thing regularly?" asked the Groolie Belkie in a puzzled manner.

"Certainly," replied the old man. "Every Christmas without fail, but I can't remember ever being down this chimney before."

"That's not surprising," said the Groolie Belkie, "seeing as it's just been built. But tell me, what's the point of this chimney business anyway?"

"Well," said the old man, "this is my good deed for the year. I visit every house at Christmas with a present. To celebrate The Birthday, you see. It's a wonderful cure for loneliness, a good deed. You should try it." "I will," said the Groolie Belkie, busying himself making supper for the old man.

For a while, the two sat comfortably in the firelight, till at last the Groolie Belkie fell fast asleep, and slept till morning. When he awoke, he was sure it had all been a dream; but as he was about to put on his sock, he felt something heavy in the toe, and out fell a shiny new knife. Here was his present from the old man – the Groolie Belkie's first Christmas present.

Then was he not delighted! He rushed out into the cold morning looking this way and that, wondering what good deed he could find to do to celebrate The Birthday.

And you may be sure he found something, because there is always an opportunity for a good deed, if you look for it, whether it's to celebrate The Birthday or not.

The Shepherd Boy's Flute

Once upon a time, long ago, before the years were numbered, there lived a peedie shepherd boy. With the older men he tended the sheep in the far fields, guiding them over the stony ways and the rough places, to find the richest pasture.

To while away the waiting hours when the sheep were peacefully grazing, he carved himself a flute and the bubbling notes blew sweetly over the rough hillside, sometimes sad and slow, and sometimes gay and wild as the mood was upon him.

Usually the days were warm and dry and bright, but with the coming of night the air grew chill and cold and the shepherds would gather their flocks together and build a fire both for warmth and for frightening away any intruder who might wish to harm the flock. By the flickering light of the flames they would huddle together to eat their supper of bread and wine, and then they would wrap themselves in their heavy cloaks and lie down tired and weary, to sleep by the fire.

The shepherd boy was always asleep long before anyone else because he was only a peedie boy and work was hard and tiring. The older men would make room for him nearest the warmth of the fire, and he'd curl up with his precious flute folded beside him in his cloak.

One night a strange thing happened. Long after the others were fast asleep, the peedie shepherd boy woke up. All the world was still, and then, high in the sky, the Merry Dancers began to glide and flicker, glowing in all the colours of the rainbow, sweeping over the roof of the sky till the earth shone in the pearly light.

The peedie shepherd boy sat up and rubbed his eyes. Far away in the wind he heard the sound of music that grew louder and clearer till the whole world rang with melody. The stars sparkled and shimmered like diamonds in the velvet sky, and hung so low that the peedie shepherd boy thought that he could almost touch them.

One star glowed brighter than the rest, its crystal rays seeming to beckon the peedie shepherd boy. He sprang up and woke his companions and the little band gazed in wonder at the glorious sight, following the brilliant star down along the stony hillside until they reached the scattered buildings on the outskirts of the town. There in a lowly stable they found a mother with her baby. She had made a bed for it among the straw, and the peedie shepherd boy saw that the baby had no warm shawl to enfold it, only a thin cloth wrapped around. His heart was filled with pity because they were so poor and he wished that he could only help the little family, but what could a poor peedie shepherd boy do?

By this time a crowd had gathered to watch and marvel, and the noise and bustle woke the sleeping baby. It began to cry and the patient mother tried in vain to soothe it. Then the peedie shepherd boy remembered his flute. He began to play softly, a sleepy song for a baby, until once more it fell asleep in the cradle of straw, the gentle notes of the flute floating up into the velvet dark.

Glossary

Aiser	Roaring (fire)	**Herdie**	Shepherd
Aisons	Eaves	**Heuk**	Hook
Bate	Beat/top	**Jumping jeck**	Sandhopper
Bhour tree	Elder tree		
Blatho	Buttermilk	**Keelieworm**	Caterpillar
Brullyo	Commotion	**Kirsty kringlick**	Field spider
Buckies	Large whelks		
		Leaped gibbo	Buttermilk with oatmeal
Chingle	Shingle	**Lickull**	Little
Corbie	Crow		
Creechurs	Creatures	**Matlo**	Bluebottle
		Moagsing	Wading through snow or mud
Dochans	Dock plants		
		Muckle	Big
Eltan	Rooting about in	**Mudgie**	Midge
Forky-tail	Earwig	**Neep**	Turnip
		Nokh	Monster
Gablo	Beetle		
Gibbo	Hot buttermilk	**Peedie**	Small
		Puddling	Paddling
Gowans	Yellow daisies		
Grimplins	Dusk/twilight	**Rootle**	Rummage
Groolie Belkie	Hideous monster		
Grullyan	Giant		

129

Segs	Rushes
Soldiers	Plantain
Spundered	Ran
Teebro	Heat shimmer
Trevallie	Crashing about
Trolling	Going
Trow	Troll
Voldro	Vole
Ware	Seaweed
Yokit	Set to/ go about something